Devil at Rocky Pointe

Devil at Rocky Pointe

The Final Stroke

On this course, par is survival.

W Mark Harrington

Disclaimer

This is a work of fiction. Names, characters, places, organizations, timelines, and events are products of the author's imagination or are used fictitiously. Any resemblance to actual persons, living or dead, or to actual events is purely coincidental. Story locations and chronology may have been adjusted to serve narrative flow.

Content Warning

This novel contains mature themes, including violence, strong language, and disturbing situations that may not be suitable for all readers. Discretion is advised.

Dedication

To my M's—my beautiful chaos, my cheer squad, and my inner compass.

Through calm days and stormy nights, you've been my anchor. Each of you carries a rhythm all your own, and together, that harmony keeps me steady. Thank you for standing by me, even when you suspected I was slipping away to chase words instead of rest. In the end, the most challenging game I played wasn't on any board; it was here, on the page. Always thinking three moves ahead, second-guessing myself, and hoping I wasn't about to land in checkmate.

P.S. Rest easy—no M's were left behind on the 18th green or in any bunker during the making of Devil at Rocky Pointe.

This Book is the second book in the
Will Anderson and Casey Murphy Series.
You can find the first book,
Demon of Oakhaven
along with
Blood and Silence: Will Anderson Origins
available at your local book retailer and online.

Table of Contents

ACKNOWLEDGEMENTS

Jordan is and will always be the GOAT!
GDTBATH

For Charlie Kirk: conviction of faith in one hand, freedom in the other, he preached what he believed and kept the forum open, protecting the liberty that lets facts breathe so that truth can stand and justice can follow.

"A killer always has the first move. Detectives live their lives trying to catch up."
— Unknown Investigator's Saying

Have nothing to do with the fruitless deeds of darkness, but rather expose them. -Ep 5:11

Prologue: Murder on the Green

Golf was supposed to be a gentleman's game.

A pale mist drifted over the manicured fairways of Lakeview at Rocky Pointe Golf Club, curling low and slow, clinging to the blades of grass as if unwilling to let go. The last of the sunset had bled into a deep violet sky, its color mirrored in the water hazards that cut through the course like dark glass. In the distance, the clubhouse glowed with warm amber light, windows lit like watchful eyes as the evening crew finished their final rounds of cleanup.

Near the eighteenth green, the soft hum of a maintenance cart broke the quiet. The lone greenskeeper—Harold Baker, fifty-three, knees aching from thirty years of keeping rich men's lawns perfect—shifted in his seat. He hated this time of evening, when the mist made even familiar shapes look wrong.

He squinted ahead.

An abandoned golf cart sat half on the fringe, half in the fairway. The headlights were dark, the keys still dangling in the ignition. No golfers. No caddies. Just that odd silhouette lying across the green.

"Hell," he muttered. "Kids again."

The shape didn't move.

He slowed the maintenance cart to a crawl, the engine's whine thinning to a nervous hum. His breath misted in the air as he eased closer, the fog thick enough now to blur the distance between night and nightmare.

At first, it looked like a mannequin—a bad prank. The country club kids had done worse. But as Harold flicked on his cart's headlights, the beam caught the sheen of something wet. The shape resolved into the pale arc of a face. And then he saw it.

The body of Charles Whitmore—club board member, wealthy, always in a pressed polo and that self-satisfied grin—lay sprawled across the green as if dropped from the sky. His face was painted an unnatural, mottled green, streaked like camouflage. A broken nine-iron jutted from his chest at a grotesque angle; the other half lay nearby, its grip slick and dark in the mist. On his gloved left hand, a blood-red Roman numeral V was slashed across the palm, uneven and raw.

Harold's breath hitched. For a second, the world seemed to tilt.

"Jesus," he whispered.

He took one step forward, then another—until he saw the eyes. Whitmore's were half-open, staring toward the clubhouse lights as if watching his own wake. Harold stumbled back, almost tripping over the lip of the cart path.

He wanted to run. Every instinct told him to. But his boots felt nailed to the turf. All he could do was stand there, heart hammering, realizing that whatever had happened here wasn't meant to stay hidden.

His hands shook as he grabbed the radio from his belt. "Clubhouse—this is Baker on the eighteen. You better— God—better send someone up here right now. We got a situation. We got a *body*."

The radio crackled back static. Then a voice, uncertain. "Say again?"

He looked once more at the green, the broken club, the mark on the glove. The mist swallowed his words.

By the time Detectives Will Anderson and Casey Murphy arrived, the fog had thickened, swallowing the edges of the green until the world felt smaller, confined. Cruiser headlights cut ribbons through the mist, turning the grass into fractured glass.

Eldon Price, the assistant greenskeeper, stood behind the rope line, cap twisting in his hands. His face was gray under the scene lights.

"We just rolled this green," he said. "Brand new cut. Look at it now."

Will stepped out of his vehicle, the wet turf giving slightly under his boots. The air smelled of fertilizer and something metallic beneath it — copper and rain. His breath came out white.

He'd seen hundreds of scenes like this in his years with Oakhaven PD, but the first one of any case always felt different — too quiet, too clean, like the calm before something starts to rot.

Detective Will Anderson moved with the deliberate patience of a man who never stopped watching. Mid-forties, weathered around the eyes, broad-shouldered from years of fieldwork. He didn't fidget, didn't rush. Even in the shifting fog, he missed nothing. The world spoke in details, and Will listened.

He stopped near the body. Charles Whitmore lay on his back, shirt torn, the red "V" across his glove glaring against the perfect green. The broken nine-iron jutted up like an accusation.

Will's jaw tightened. *Always something ugly hiding under perfect turf.*

A figure moved through the mist behind him. Detective Casey Murphy ducked under the rope line, the beam of her flashlight cutting across the scene. She was tall, athletic, with her red hair pulled back in a loose knot that the fog had already started to undo. Her green eyes caught the light — sharp, piercing, impatient.

"Guess the country club's annual charity drive got interesting," she said, crouching beside the body.

Her tone was easy, but her eyes weren't. Casey Murphy didn't believe in quiet nights — she believed in finding what the quiet was hiding.

Will gave her a sidelong glance. "You always have to start with sarcasm?"

"Coping mechanism." She snapped on her gloves. "You should try one sometime."

"Mine's silence."

"I noticed," she muttered, kneeling beside the corpse.

Will smirked faintly, then refocused on the scene. Casey had been his partner for three years — long enough that he could read her moods by the angle of her shoulders. Bull-headed, quick to challenge, sharper than most rookies he'd ever broken in. She had instincts—raw and fast, while his worked slower—deliberate, connective, like the click of gears. Together, they made sense of chaos.

Casey leaned in close, flashlight hovering over Whitmore's glove. "Roman numeral," she murmured. "Or just a letter. V."

Will crouched beside her. "First move... or final one?"

"Depends." Her green eyes flicked up through the mist. "You think our guy's climbing the scoreboard — or running out of holes?"

He didn't answer. The fog was thick now, rolling low, swallowing the lights until the scene looked like a stage meant for ghosts. He'd been on enough of these to feel the pulse of something methodical, something planned.

"Call it in," he said quietly. "Tell Monroe we'll need the M.E., forensics, and a full scene light setup."

Casey stood, brushing condensation off her knees. "You think this connects to—"

"I think someone's keeping score," Will said, crouching again beside the corpse. The broken shaft gleamed faintly in his flashlight. "And we just found the scorecard."

Casey smirked faintly. "Maybe someone lost big in their skins game and didn't pay up."

"Who knows?"

"Still," she said, looking down at the wound, "whoever did this wasn't just angry. That's overkill. That's personal."

Will didn't respond. His light swept over the corpse's face, tracing the green streaks that shimmered faintly under the beam. It wasn't random splatter. It was applied deliberately.

He leaned closer, the cold mist collecting on his collar. "What the hell is with the paint?"

Casey tilted her head, frowning. "Not turf paint. That's something else, but weird doesn't do it justice."

Will straightened slowly, the smell of the scene—wet grass, metal, rot—settling in his lungs. His pulse beat once, hard, as recognition flickered.

Too deliberate. Too familiar.

He'd seen something like this before.

And last time, it hadn't stopped at one.

Clubhouse Whispers

Inside the clubhouse, the chandeliers glimmered like trapped stars, scattering fractured light across marble floors. The air carried the faint scent of polish and expensive aftershave – clean, sharp, trying too hard.

Club members huddled in small groups throughout the lounge and restaurant, their voices lowered but urgent. Conversations fluttered like nervous wings, all questions and speculation. The laughter that normally filled the bar was gone, replaced by the hush of money realizing it might be implicated.

Graham Holloway stood apart, one shoulder against a limestone column, a tumbler of Glenlivet warming in his hand. He hadn't taken a sip. The whiskey was comfort; tonight it was just weight.

Across the room, Elliot Carrington, the club's general manager, moved through the knots of members with a politician's smile and the tension of a man trapped between power and damage control. Every sentence sounded like a press release.

"No, I'm afraid I can't comment on Mr. Whitmore's current status with the board," Carrington said for the third time, his tone dipped in honey and panic.

Colleen Morris, wrapped in pale cashmere, gave a tight smile.

"But he chaired the finance committee. Surely that's relevant."

Carrington's jaw clenched; his smile didn't.

"That was... some time ago."

He checked his watch — a reflex. Guilty people always did.

Holloway watched him the way he'd once watched suspects — steady, unblinking. Whitmore's name, engraved on half the trophies in the case beside him, caught the light. He ran a fingertip over one. The metal was cold.

Whitmore had been a loud man — not in volume but presence. You didn't erase a man like that overnight. If Carrington was dodging, it wasn't to save the club's reputation. It was to save his own.

Holloway set his glass down and followed as Carrington slipped toward the hallway.

"Mr. Holloway," Carrington said, startled when he turned. His smile wavered. "Now isn't—"

"Save it," Holloway interrupted. "You were outside."

"Everyone was."

"Not everyone has damp grass on their trousers."

Carrington glanced down at his cuff — a faint green smear, almost invisible under the light. He recovered quickly.

"The police asked me to show them the terrace approach. Routine."

"Routine's the sprinklers coming on at five a.m. daily," Holloway said. "This isn't that."

Carrington exhaled slowly. "You're upset."

"No," Holloway said, stepping closer. "I'm observant. And I know Whitmore. This mess — it has his shape."

"We're closing early," Carrington said, angling toward the staff corridor.

Holloway blocked him with half a step.

"Colleen asked about the finance committee. You dodged."

"I answered."

"You dodged," Holloway repeated, voice like gravel. "When did Whitmore step off?"

Carrington's eyes flicked — quick, instinctive — toward a framed audit certificate on the wall.

"He scaled back last year."

"Or got pushed. There's a difference. One shows up in the books."

A faint hum filled the silence — the ice machine in the bar. Outside the tall windows, blue-and-red light from the police cruisers pulsed against the fog, painting the marble in nervous color.

On the eighteenth green, just beyond the terrace, Whitmore's body lay in the mist. Holloway didn't need to look; he'd seen it reflected in the lights from the officers earlier — the glove, the red V.

"You see that mark?" Holloway asked softly. "The V."

Carrington's nostrils flared. "I see the police doing their jobs."

"V for what? Visitor? Victor?"

"Vice," Carrington said too fast. Then, with a shrug, "Could be a glove brand. I don't golf much."

Holloway almost laughed. "You play twice a week."

"Not lately."

Holloway leaned in, voice low. "Whitmore hated monograms. Called them talismans for men with something to hide."

Carrington's composure cracked — just for a breath.

Down the hallway, the locker room door stood slightly ajar, a strip of yellow tape clinging to the hinge.

"You left it open," Holloway said quietly. "Keypad bypassed. That's coordination."

"Mr. Holloway, it's best to let the police handle this."

"They will," Holloway said. "Question is, when they're done, what will you be — cooperative or interesting?"

He left Carrington standing in the corridor and walked toward the trophy case again, tapping a finger against the glass over Whitmore's name.

"He didn't fall quietly," Holloway murmured. "Men like him never do."

The hum of conversation faded as he drifted toward the locker room. The door creaked open; the air inside smelled of eucalyptus and damp wool. On the bench: a neatly folded towel, a dark V-shaped smear wet across the fabric.

His pulse stayed steady. He'd been a reserve deputy once — old habits die last. But this wasn't just curiosity.

This was instinct.

Only members have access to the locker room.

He shut the door softly. Somewhere outside, the flash of another camera lit the fog.

A chill moved through him.

Outside, the mist rolled thick across the eighteenth, diffusing the cruiser lights into pale ghosts. Through the clubhouse windows, Holloway's reflection dissolved into the fog. Below, the detectives worked methodically, small figures against the green.

On the 18th green, the air hummed with quiet purpose — cameras clicking, radios murmuring, footsteps muffled in wet grass.

Detective Will Anderson stood at the fringe of the green, his gaze tracking the measured rhythm of the forensics team. Every scene started as chaos; his job was to find the pattern. Tonight, it felt like the pattern was watching him back.

Beside him, Casey Murphy shifted her stance, arms crossed. Her copper hair caught the spill of floodlight, the color alive against the mist.

"Captain's here," she murmured.

Will followed her gaze. Captain Frank Monroe approached, hands in pockets, expression unreadable. He was new to Oakhaven, fresh from a larger city, his voice even and direct.

"Look, Anderson," Monroe said. "I'm not your last captain. I won't micromanage. Keep me in the loop, do your job, and I'll keep the mayor off your back. Deal?"

Will nodded. "Deal."

Monroe gave a curt nod and moved toward the onlookers near the rope line.

Casey leaned in. "Not sure if I like him yet."

"Give it time," Will said. "He'll either keep his word or he won't."

From near the golf cart, a young tech straightened. "Detectives," he called, holding up a sealed evidence bag. Inside: a crisp scorecard, a slash of red ink cutting across the center.

One down. Par is never enough.

Casey stared at it, her tone dry. "Well, that's comforting."

Will studied the handwriting — blocky, deliberate. "He's keeping score," he said quietly.

Casey looked at him. "You think we're on it yet?"

Will didn't answer.

The wind shifted, carrying the faint scent of rain and cut grass from the terrace above. Somewhere behind them, a camera flash burst through the mist, stark white.

Will's phone buzzed in his pocket — **Kristen.**

He let it ring.

If the killer was keeping score, the only question that mattered now was simple.

Who's next on the card?

The DA's Warning

The TV glowed in the dim kitchen, casting flickers of light across the countertops. Onscreen, late-night news anchors spoke with that brisk, detached cadence reserved for violent headlines.

A live shot from Lakeview at Rocky Pointe Golf Club filled the screen—crime scene tape rippling in the mist, cruisers idling behind it, headlights cutting through the fog. A close-up of Detectives Will Anderson and Casey Murphy flashed across the screen. They were still on site.

Kristen stood frozen in front of the television, one hand wrapped around a mug long gone cold. She barely heard the anchor's words. She felt them—in the tightness in her chest, the quickening pulse, the memory-tinged dread curling beneath her ribs.

Kristen hung up the phone, laying it on the counter. Will was too busy to answer.

Her free hand drifted to her shoulder. Fingers brushed the faint scar beneath her sweater, a reflex born from scars deeper than skin.

From the hallway came the clack of phone keys.

Ellie's voice floated in, half-amused: "Whoa, the country club? Fancy. Bet this'll blow up on Insta."

Kristen turned. Her voice was sharper than she meant. "Ellie. That's not funny."

Ellie looked up, confused. "Nobody gets murdered on a golf course," she said. "It's like *Clue*—but with golf carts."

Kristen didn't blink. "This isn't a game."

She turned back to the TV, steadying her breath, heart still ticking faster than it should.

Ellie shrugged and drifted off. A few minutes later, she posted a filtered screenshot of the glowing green, mist curling around the lights like a ghost. Her caption: *Oakhaven's got its own Agatha Christie now.*

Kristen didn't see the post. She didn't need to.

Some things, you feel before they happen—in the weight of old wounds, in silences that don't pass.

The Gala – Memory Flashback

She stayed rooted to the news feed, eyes locked on Whitmore's image—posed in death beneath stadium lights.

Her memory slipped back: the gala, polished floors, champagne laughter. Whitmore drifting through the crowd like he owned the oxygen. He'd caught her by the elbow near the donor wall.

His smile had been soft. His eyes had not.

"I make it my business to know things," he said. "You should think about being careful."

"Careful about what?" she'd asked.

He glanced toward a tight circle of board members.

"Where you step," he said. "In Oakhaven, reputations are lawns. Pretty from the cart path. Tear up the turf, people notice."

He'd rolled a divot tool between his fingers, then slipped it into his jacket pocket with a wink that never reached his eyes.

Back then, it had sounded like advice. Now, watching him dead on a golf green, it sounded like something else:

Not a warning.

A reminder.

Clubhouse Terrace – Present

Will stepped away from the hum of the scene, into the shadows beneath the clubhouse terrace. The wind carried the scent of wet turf and rain-soaked azaleas. Below, the eighteenth green gleamed in the mist, ringed with yellow tape, too quiet.

His phone buzzed again.

Kristen.

This time, he answered. "Hey, honey."

"Not a social call," she said.

Her voice was calm, measured—but Will knew that edge. It was the one she used in trial prep, when pressure built and her words honed to a blade. Not rattled. Just ready.

"I've been following the news feed," she said. "This thing on the green? It's not about golf."

Will leaned against the stone railing. Below, Casey crouched near the cart path, where a tech held up an evidence bag—the scorecard catching the light.

"Go on."

"There are names tied to Whitmore," Kristen said. "Same ones from the Oakhaven contracts scandal. Finance committee. The April 14th vote—they all signed off."

Will's brow furrowed. "The vote that triggered the audit?"

"Exactly. But there's more. Unfiled allegations—sexual misconduct, another board member. Nothing made it to court, but it circulated. And it was ugly. Epstein-level ugly. Just with better suits and country club silence."

Will's jaw tightened.

"And now," Kristen said, "Steve's in a cell. But don't assume he's finished."

"You think he's still pulling strings?"

"I think influence doesn't vanish just because the door locks." A beat. He heard the faint click of her pen, that nervous rhythm she always slipped into when her thoughts raced ahead of her mouth.

"If this story grows legs," she said, "the whole board could go down. And if that happens? This isn't a sideshow. It's the main act. Starting early."

Will glanced at the scorecard in the bag. The red ink cut across it like a wound:

ONE DOWN. PAR IS NEVER ENOUGH.

His voice was low. "We'll see who's keeping score."

Kristen's voice was quieter. Almost lost to the wind.
"Just make sure you're not on the card."

The kitchen faucet ran hot, steam curling upward as Ellie rinsed two mugs. From the hall came Kristen's voice—low, clipped, urgent.

Ellie wasn't trying to eavesdrop, but the old house carried sound like secrets.

She caught fragments.

Her dad's name.

Old cases.

And then:

"Just because he's locked up doesn't mean his influence is."

Her hand stilled under the stream. The water burned across her knuckles.

Footsteps approached.

The conversation cut off mid-sentence.

Kristen appeared in the doorway, phone still in hand, her expression carefully neutral.

"You okay?" she asked.

Ellie shut off the tap and grabbed a dish towel, buying herself a beat.

"Yeah. I, uh... I saw something online earlier."

Kristen's brow lifted—polite, but guarded. "Yeah?"

"It was one of those weird sermon videos people pass around. Bad lighting, tiny pulpit. Real fringe-church stuff."

Kristen stepped into the room, setting her phone down with a soft click.

"What was it about?"

"He was quoting Bible verses," Ellie said. "But they were... twisted. Not wrong exactly, just off. Like someone cut them apart and glued the pieces back together wrong, one line stuck out: 'One down.' Like it was Old Testament or something, but—more threat than blessing."

Kristen tilted her head. "Do you remember which book?"

Ellie shook her head. "No. Just that it sounded familiar, like I've seen that phrase before, but I can't place it."

She glanced at her phone. "Weird thing is... someone tagged me in a picture from the pier." She frowned. "Only—I wasn't there that day."

She shrugged it off, but her thumb kept scrolling.

Kristen said nothing. Just silence—and that moment stretched a little too long.

She gave a small smile, warm enough to pass but not quite real.

"If you find it again," Kristen said, "send me the link."

Ellie nodded, but her hands tightened around the towel.

The moment clung like static.

It wasn't the sermon that felt wrong.

It was Kristen's voice when she said *book*.

It was the way her smile never quite reached her eyes.

Second Body, Second Clue

The crime-scene tech was still photographing the green when the door to the pro shop banged open from the inside.

A uniformed officer jogged across the damp grass, breath fogging in the cold, radio crackling faintly on his shoulder.

"Detectives—another body," he said, chest heaving. "Over by the driving range."

Will and Casey straightened. The fatigue that had been creeping in vanished, replaced by the sharp focus that only bad news could bring.

"Same staging?" Will asked.

"Identical." The officer's tone was grim. "Golf glove on the left hand. Black paint. This one says VI."

Casey frowned. "V, now VI." She looked back toward the eighteenth. "Roman numerals. Feels less like a message..." Her eyes narrowed. "More like a score."

Will's voice stayed flat. "Who?"

"Thomas Gilmore. Finance committee—same as Whitmore. Retired banker. Member here for thirty years. Grounds crew found him slumped against the fence by the ball dispensers." The officer hesitated, lowering his voice. "He used to serve with Whitmore... right up until the audit."

Will met Casey's gaze. The pattern wasn't just numbers—it was names. And those names were starting to rhyme.

Through the fog-smeared glass of the clubhouse, the distant floodlights pulsed like a heartbeat. Somewhere beyond the rows of tee-off mats waited another body, another mark in someone's private game.

A kill list.

A countdown.

And they were entering mid-round.

They crossed the damp stretch toward the range, beams from the floodlights carving hard lines through the mist. The smell of wet turf and cut rubber from the mats mixed with the faint tang of oil from the ball dispensers.

Two uniforms waited by the tape. Beyond them, Thomas Gilmore was propped against the chain-link fence, knees bent as if he'd sat to rest. Only the angle of his head—and the deep, jagged cut across his throat—told the truth. Whoever had done this hadn't been gentle. The wound looked sawed more than sliced.

The white golf glove on his left hand gleamed under the lights, the thick black VI painted across the palm still glossy with moisture. Just above the Velcro tab was a streak of red ink—the same crimson tone as the note on the scorecard inside the clubhouse.

Casey crouched beside the body, flashlight steady. "Whitmore. Gilmore." She exhaled softly. "Guess the next guy's Happy. Tell me I'm wrong."

Will didn't smile. "Gilmore doesn't look happy."

"Not a fan of the long-drive competition, huh?" she said, standing. Her breath clouded in the cold.

One of the uniforms gave a nervous half-chuckle and then remembered himself.

Will slipped on gloves, leaned in closer. "Same paint, same handwriting style. Whoever staged this touched the glove after writing that note." He stared at the ink, thinking how deliberate it looked—ritual over rage.

Casey's gaze followed the fog toward the range's far edge. "You think the V and VI are counting up or down?"

"Five, six..." she murmured. "Feels like we're walking into the middle of the round."

Will's jaw tightened. "Only if he's playing straight." A pause. "He's not. This isn't by the book—it's by his rules."

"So, not in order," she said quietly. "Just the victims he wants, when he wants."

Will's eyes swept the dark fairway beyond the tape. "Either way, the next number's coming faster than we want."

Somewhere out in the mist, a sprinkler hissed to life, water arcing silver in the floodlight. The rhythmic spray ticked like a metronome in the silence, measuring time they didn't have.

At the Anderson house, the night felt heavier. Ellie sat curled on the couch, blanket wrapped around her knees, the glow of her phone painting her face a cold blue. When her twin sister, Emily, walked in, balancing two mugs of hot chocolate, the air smelled faintly of cinnamon and rain drifting through the cracked window.

"Hey," Emily said, setting the mugs on the coffee table. "You've been glued to that thing all night. Everything okay?"

Ellie turned the screen toward her. A blog headline blared in red:

Driving Range Death: Rocky Pointe Country Club Member Found Late Friday Night.

Below it, a grainy photo of Thomas Gilmore—probably lifted from some old committee dinner. Emily frowned. "PD hasn't released a name yet. How—?"

"It's on a message board," Ellie said quickly, too quickly. "They crowdsource from scanner chatter, eyewitness stuff. Not official-official."

Emily scrolled down, eyes catching on a username: BookofNumbersV6.
The post beneath it read:

The grass grows lush where the righteous pretend.
They manicure their sins like fairways
neat, trimmed, unseen.
But rot does not respect country clubs.
The tee box is the altar.
The swing is confession.
And the hole? Judgment.
I count not scores, but strokes.
Each number is a name. Each name, a weight.
And I will lift them, one by one.
Par is never enough.

Emily's stomach tightened. "That's... creepy. Is that supposed to be a Bible verse?"

"Not exactly." Ellie's voice dropped. "They post twisted out-of-context stuff like that sometimes. Just ignore it."

Emily looked up sharply. "Ellie, that was posted twenty minutes ago. Have they even finished clearing the scene? That's too fast."

Ellie's thumb hovered over the screen before she locked it and dropped the phone into her lap. "It's just people talking," she said. "Doesn't mean they're right."

But the uncertainty in her voice betrayed her. Emily saw it—the flicker that meant her sister knew more than she was saying.

"Be careful with that," Emily said quietly. "Fast information usually comes from people who need it out there."

Ellie didn't reply. Outside, a siren wailed somewhere distant, fading north into the mist. The living room fell still except for the hum of the refrigerator and the faint drip of rain at the window—steady, rhythmic, like a countdown.

Forensic Echo

The deputy coroner, medical examiner, stood near the edge of the range, a disposable coverall crinkling with each shift of her weight. Her gloved hands gestured to the body as the CSU team packed their kits.

"Both victims were killed elsewhere," she said, voice even. "No blood pooling here, no drag marks, lividity is all wrong. They were posed postmortem, deliberately, and with time to spare." She pointed toward the glove. "And whoever handled this knew exactly how to make it look staged without smearing the paint."

Casey crouched to study the black numeral again. "Speaking of paint—what's in it? It looks strange."

The ME gave a slight shrug. "Chemical presumptive test swab came back with traces of a rare polymer compound, the same base as the white enamel used in the Oakhaven murders just a while ago. The home lab will be able to tell for sure. But the dry texture, it looks and smells the same, with the same weird smell." She looked at them over the rim of her mask. "Cain's signature," the ME said. "Right down to the chemical scent."

Will felt his shoulders stiffen. Julien Cain, the sadistic perfectionist whose trophies had been displayed like art pieces, was sitting in the county lockup awaiting trial on state and federal charges.

"Cain's still in custody," Casey said slowly. "So either someone got hold of his supply..."

"Or someone's sending a message," Will finished.

They stood there a moment, eyes locked over Gilmore's body, the pulsing floodlights strobing in the fog.

"This isn't a coincidence," Casey said.

"No," Will agreed, his voice low. "It's an invitation."

The ME moved off toward her van, leaving the two detectives in the glare of the floodlights. Will's eyes stayed on the ink smear above the glove's cuff, same shade, same deliberate touch as the scorecard.

Casey broke the silence. "Cain's been in county lockup for a while now. The only way this paint shows up here is if somebody got close enough to him to get a sample, or he told them exactly where to find it."

Will's jaw tightened. "Which means they've been in the same room."

She glanced toward the CSU truck. "Visitor logs."

"Yeah," Will said, already pulling out his phone. "If anyone sat across from Cain in the last six months, I want their name, their address, and a reason why they're still breathing."

Casey arched a brow. "And if it's someone we already know?"

"Then we find out how many more numbers they've got left to paint."

The wind shifted, carrying the faint scent of wet turf and oil from the ball dispensers. Somewhere downrange, a sprinkler hissed in the darkness, steady as a metronome.

Julien Cain – Ravenwood County Detention Center

The county jail visiting room was always too cold, the kind of chill that sank into the bones. Fluorescents buzzed overhead, pale light pooling on scratched metal tables bolted to the floor.

Will sat at one of them, shoulders squared, arms crossed, his gaze fixed on the door. Casey leaned back in her chair, one boot tapping a quiet rhythm against the linoleum, restless energy betraying her calm mask.

The door opened with a hydraulic hiss. Julien Cain strolled in like he'd been announced, chains clinking faintly at his wrists. Even in the orange jumpsuit, he carried himself like a man auditioning for applause — spine straight, chin lifted, eyes gleaming with a predator's calm.

"Detectives." Cain lowered himself into the chair as though granting an audience. His cuffs clinked softly against the table. "To what do I owe the pleasure?"

Casey didn't waste time. She leaned forward, palms flat on the table. "Someone's staging murders with your paint. Same compound. Same precision. Tell me I'm wrong."

Cain's smile tugged slowly and deliberately. "And you think I've been sneaking out nights?"

Will leaned in, forearms braced against steel. His voice was flat, low. "Not nights. Visitors."

Cain's gaze flicked between them, measuring, savoring. "Ah. You've seen my logs." His fingers drummed once on the table, a lazy rhythm that carried too much intent.

"Who are they?" Casey pressed.

Cain shrugged, the motion elegant despite the jumpsuit. He leaned back, the chair legs groaning in protest. "Attorneys. Public defenders. A journalist who thought he could profile me. A chaplain who couldn't quote Leviticus to save his soul. None that would interest you."

Will slid a photocopy across the table. The paper whispered against the steel. One name circled in red. "This one. Twice in the last three months. Over an hour each time. Who is it?"

Cain let his eyes linger on the page. His smile widened, deliberate, calculated to irritate. "A student," he murmured. "Everyone needs someone to carry on their work. You train a hand, you train an eye... and one day, they surpass you."

Casey's voice was sharp, cutting. "Your student is painting Roman numerals on golf gloves."

Cain's head tilted slightly, like a curator considering a canvas. His voice dropped, smooth as velvet. "Art evolves. Mediums change. Messages shift. But the signature—" His eyes locked with Will's, unblinking. "The signature is eternal."

Will's jaw flexed, the muscles ticking once. "Name."

Cain's chuckle was soft, almost intimate—like he was sharing a private joke meant only for them. Then silence stretched, thick and suffocating.

"Tell me, Detective," Cain finally said, leaning forward until the chains bit into his wrists. His smile was all teeth now. "How many numbers have you seen so far?"

Will didn't answer.

Cain's grin widened, wolfish, savoring the moment. He leaned back slowly, the cuffs scraping across the tabletop like a blade on stone. "Then your education," he whispered, "is just beginning."

Cain and Leary First Meeting

He hadn't thought about that day in months.

Marcus Leary remembered the way Cain spoke the first time they met face-to-face, not like a prisoner, but like a high priest anointing an initiate.

"The world doesn't bleed anymore, Marcus," Cain had said, his voice smooth and low, eyes shining behind the scratched plexiglass. "It decays in silence. We are the ones who must give it voice again."

Marcus had leaned forward, barely breathing.

"They call it madness," Cain continued, "but we know better. We don't kill. We compose. We create moments of reckoning. Beautiful, precise. For the unbelievers to find and tremble."

He had tapped the table gently, three times. "Few are called. Fewer understand. But you, Marcus, you see it, don't you? The pattern beneath the skin. The truth behind the score."

Marcus had nodded. That was the moment he knew: he wasn't alone. He wasn't lost. He was being invited into a rarified club, one whose membership came not with a handshake, but with a signature in red.

Back at the Office

The late-night hum of the bullpen was quieter than usual, with most of the desks dark. Will leaned against his, arms crossed, holding the visitor log printout. The circled name, Marcus Leary, looked like a stain on the page. Casey stood near the whiteboard, eyes scanning the list of finance committee members they had tacked up in the last hour.

"We've got at least a half-dozen people who sat on that committee with Whitmore and Gilmore," Casey said. "And now we've got Leary. He visits Cain twice, disappears for a week at a time, and somehow has ties to three of these names."

Will's voice was low, clipped. "We don't go public. Not yet. We're not sure it's Leary."

Casey shot back, sharp. "And if he paints another Roman numeral while we hesitate?" Casey snapped. What do we tell their family, that we were worried about optics?"

Will didn't blink. "We'll see. Caution keeps him close."

Casey leaned in. "Caution keeps the morgue busy."

"I'm saying we move carefully," Will replied. "We don't know the order. For all we know, 'V' and 'VI' are random. Leary might be playing a totally different game."

"Or he could be sitting in his car outside the next target's house right now."

Will dropped the printout on his desk, the circled name glaring up at both of them. "We have to be sure before we make this public. If we tip him off, we may never get close again." Casey stared at the name, then back at Will.

"So we wait until we're sure... and hope the body count doesn't go any higher." Will exhaled. "No.

We split the difference, a quiet outreach to the top three most likely targets. No official warning, no press release.

We give them just enough to take precautions without starting a stampede." Casey's gaze returned to the circled name.

"If Leary's really Cain's student, we're already three moves behind him."

Will met her eyes. "Then we'd better start catching up."

Now, looking at Cain's name circled in red, Will knew the rot hadn't started; it had been planted.

Holloway Interview

The precinct's interview room was designed to make people sweat—gray walls, a humming vent, and a table bolted to the floor.

But Graham Holloway sat as if it were his office. Blazer pressed. Posture relaxed. Eyes sharp.

Will set the file down without opening it. "Appreciate you coming in."

Holloway smirked. "You didn't ask. You summoned. Old law enforcement trick—make it sound voluntary."

Casey leaned against the wall, arms crossed. "You worked with the sheriff's office, didn't you?"

"Reserve deputy," Holloway said smoothly. "A younger man's hobby. I learned enough to know when I'm being boxed." He nodded toward the untouched water bottle. "You'll let me talk myself in circles, look for cracks. Standard drill."

Will didn't take the bait. "You were on the terrace the night Whitmore died. What did you see?"

"What I always see," Holloway replied. "What no one else notices."

He ticked it off on his fingers. "Carrington's cuff had damp grass on it — but he swore he never left the balcony."

The locker room door had tape on the lock.

"And Whitmore..." He let the name hang a beat. "Whitmore was surprised by his attacker."

31

Casey frowned. "That's what you noticed?"

"That's what matters." Holloway sat back, folding his hands. "A man like Whitmore doesn't get caught off guard–ever. Unless someone knows exactly where to push, you think it's random? It's not. Someone's keeping score. And Whitmore?" He shrugged. "He was just the opening drive."

Will studied him. "So whose move was it, yours?"

For the first time, Holloway's smile faded. "That's the wrong question, Detective. The right one is–who else at Rocky Pointe is playing?"

A pause filled the air.

"Because I promise you, I'm not the only one keeping notes."

He tapped the table once. A crisp, deliberate sound.

"But you already knew that. Didn't you?"

He stood smoothly. "I'm pretty sure you're done with me."

Casey pushed off the wall. "No more questions–for now."

Holloway smiled again, polite but empty. "Then you know where to find me. Same as they do."

The Past Creeps Back

Will was halfway through typing an incident summary when his phone lit up with a familiar name, *Rivers – DHS*. He answered on the second ring.

"Will, it's Evan Rivers," the voice came, brisk and without preamble. "We've been combing through the evidence you handed over from Steve's case. That 'tech guy' who ran the comms and encryption for the trafficking ring? He's still out there."

Reports of drugged female students from nearby colleges. No IDs, no suspects. Victims returned to dorms or apartments with gaps in memory, clothed but things out of place.

Will frowned. "We thought Dan Rogers fit that bill."

"Rogers was just a pawn," Rivers said flatly. "A glorified caretaker. They used his place as a secondary processing stage, moving the kids through, using them for their jollies, cleaning them up, then handing them off to the next sadist. The real tech operator stayed in the shadows. That's who we're after."

Will reached for a pen, already scribbling on a legal pad. "You've got a name?"

"Not yet. But we've got something else, a financial trail. Looks like the Rocky Pointe Country Club's accounts are running more cash than they should. I'm talking cartel money, laundered through the same shell companies tied to Steve's network."

Will's gaze slid to the case board, where Whitmore's photo sat next to Gilmore's, and a fresh sticky note marked *Marcus Leary*. "If you're right, then our dead bankers weren't just victims. They were part of the plumbing."

"That's my read," Rivers said. "Find the leak, you might find your tech guy. And Will... if this person's still out there, they're going to be careful. Anyone poking too hard around the club is going to get noticed."

Back at the Anderson Home

Across town, Ellie sat cross-legged on her bed, laptop balanced on her thighs, phone buzzing with notifications. Her friends-only post was already thirty comments deep.

Ugh, sick of these rich creeps at the country club acting like they own the whole damn town. Money doesn't make you untouchable! It just makes you think your crap doesn't stink.

She hit refresh, half-smiling at the snark piling up in the replies.

What she didn't know, what no one under thirty ever seemed to remember, was how fast a "friends-only" rant could leak in a place like Oakhaven. By morning, a screen-capped version would be bouncing between PTA moms, committee members... and the same club regulars she'd just skewered.

Somewhere in that chain, the wrong set of eyes would read her words, eyes that already knew exactly who she was.

That Somewhere was in the lamplit back room of the Lakeview at Rocky Point Golf Club, a laptop screen glowed in the dim. The social feed was open to a blurry screenshot of Ellie's post, her profile photo circled in red by someone's cursor.

The man in the leather chair read her words twice, the corner of his mouth ticking up in something that wasn't quite a smile. He clicked over to another window, a spreadsheet filled with names, dates, and cryptic notes.

Scrolling halfway down, he found the Anderson name, highlighted in pale yellow. He tapped the key with one finger, adding a single line to the end of her row:

Knows too much. Watch closely.

In the silence of the room, the faint hum of a small printer started up. A single page slid into the tray, her profile picture, her rant, and the date.

He slid the page into a slim folder already stuffed with similar sheets and closed it with care, like tucking something valuable out of sight.

Outside, the wind rattled the clubhouse doors.

Outside the Leary House

The unmarked SUV's headlights washed over a peeling white porch and a yard gone to seed. Plastic flamingos leaned like drunks in the mud. Beyond them, a single light glowed in the basement window — steady, low, and wrong.

Will shut off the engine. The sudden silence felt heavier than the ride over.

Casey leaned forward, eyes narrowing at the flicker in the window. "So this is him. The pen pal."

Will nodded, flipping open the thin case file in his lap. The pages were creased from too many reads. "Marcus Leary, twenty-six. Still lives with his mother. No priors. But prison mail logs show he's been writing to Julien Cain for almost a year."

Casey gave a low whistle. "Most people collect baseball cards. This guy collects murderers."

"Cain answered him," Will said. "Four times that we know of. Two letters redacted, one destroyed, one missing."

Her eyebrows lifted. "And the missing one?"

"Showed up three weeks ago. Addressed to Leary. Postmark from inside Ravenwood Detention." Will closed the file. "Cain's handwriting."

Casey leaned back in her seat, staring at the house. "You think Cain trained him?"

"I think Cain talked, he's been to see him twice," Will said. "And Leary listened."

They sat in silence for a moment. The only sound was the ticking engine and the faint rattle of wind through the gutter.

Casey finally exhaled. "You know, when we caught Cain, I thought that door was shut for good."

"Cain never shuts doors," Will said quietly. "He leaves them cracked."

A shadow passed behind the basement curtain — slow, deliberate.

Casey's hand dropped to her holster. "Looks like someone's home."

Will nodded once and opened the door. Cold air swept in, carrying the scent of rain and fried food.

They crunched up the gravel path, boots sinking slightly in the mud. The house loomed small and hunched, the kind of place that had never known laughter.

The porch light buzzed overhead as Will pressed the doorbell.

After a long moment, the door creaked open. A woman stood there in a faded robe, hair pinned back, eyes darting between their badges and their faces.

"Mrs. Leary?" Will asked.

She nodded quickly, voice soft and uncertain. "Yes. Is something wrong?"

Will held her gaze, his tone calm but edged with purpose. "We're here to speak with your son, Marcus. Is he home?"

Her fingers twisted at the sleeve of her robe. "He's... downstairs." A beat. "Marcus spends most of his time down there. He's... creative."

Casey tilted her head, eyes flicking past the woman toward the dim hallway. "Creative how?"

Mrs. Leary hesitated, the kind of pause that came from equal parts shame and fear. "You'll see," she said finally. "He doesn't like to be disturbed."

Will and Casey exchanged a look that said the same thing: *Creative never means good news.*

She stepped aside, and the smell hit them—old carpet, grease, and something faintly metallic underneath.

They followed her down the narrow stairs.

Casey's eyes narrowed. "Well, this looks familiar."

Will moved to the desk, lifting a notebook filled with jagged block handwriting. Verses copied verbatim from Cain's old files. Obsessive. Perfectly preserved.

Will lifted a stack of envelopes off the corner of the desk. The handwriting was blocky and deliberate, with the return addresses clipped clean. He frowned.

"Fan mail?" Casey asked, leaning over his shoulder.

Marcus's cheeks flushed. "Just... letters. I write. He doesn't answer back."

Casey dropped the envelopes back onto the pile with a snap. "And you keep every one. Cute."

Will's jaw tightened. "Julien Cain doesn't need to write back. He already owns you."

"All this work for a wannabe Sith apprentice who never even made it to training camp." Casey jested.

Will mutters: "So he's not the chosen one." *Casey smirks:* "Not even close."

Behind them, Marcus shuffled out of a bathroom, pale and sweating. "I know what this looks like," he stammered.

"It looks like you've been writing our crime scenes before they happen," Will said.

Marcus's gaze darted between them. "I never, I didn't..." He swallowed hard. "I just studied Cain's work," Marcus said quickly. "He's a genius, the way he staged things—"

Casey cut him off. "You've been in touch."

Marcus's fingers twitched on the edge of his desk. "No! Just letters. He never replied."

Will took a step closer, eyes scanning the cluttered workspace. Jars of paint lined the shelf — whites, greens, and one thick jar of black enamel labeled in sloppy marker. His gaze caught on a streak of the same shade across a piece of cardboard.

"You've got the same paint compound," Will said, voice low. "Exact chemical base as what we found on Whitmore and Gilmore's gloves. It isn't sold retail anymore. Cain used it to mark his victims."

Marcus swallowed hard. "I didn't—I just mixed what he mentioned in his letters. He said it was cleaner. Permanent."

Before Will could press him, the stairs creaked behind them.

Marcus's mother stood at the bottom step, clutching the railing, her knuckles white. "Detective," she said, breathless. "Marcus hasn't left this house in weeks. You're wrong about him. He was here the night those men died. I made him dinner myself. The night of—" she hesitated, voice catching, "—the fourteenth, wasn't it?"

Will turned toward her slowly. "You've been following the case."

Her eyes darted to the jars on the shelf, then back to Marcus. "It's a small town, Detective. People talk."

Casey's glance flicked toward Will. *The date. She knew the date.*

The air thickened between them, heavy with paint fumes and something worse—fear.

Silence hung, thick and ugly.

Casey glanced around the room one more time — the gloves on the wall, the pinned scorecards, the Roman numerals scrawled across cardboard. It was all theater. Disturbing, but not deadly.

She exhaled slowly. "He's not our guy."

Marcus's voice cracked, too eager, too desperate. "But I could be. If Cain showed me how."

Will's eyes went cold. "That's exactly the problem." He stepped closer, lowering his voice. "You think men like Cain *teach* something worth learning? He doesn't make artists. He makes echoes. Parasites who mistake imitation for purpose. You think he saw you as a student? He saw a mirror — one he could crack and leave grinning back at him. Cain is a sick, low-life pervert. You want to be that?"

Marcus blinked, trembling, his fingers stained with black enamel.

Will's voice stayed level, steady as a blade. "Cain doesn't recruit killers. He manufactures excuses. Don't let him finish the job."

Silence stretched. Only the hum of the basement light filled the space.

Then Casey broke it, flatly: "We're done here."

They turned for the stairs. Marcus didn't move, just watched them go, his mouth forming words too soft to hear.

Outside, the night air hit hard. Casey slammed the car door harder than necessary. "Two days," she muttered. "We just wasted two days chasing a man-child in his mother's basement."

Will didn't respond right away. His gaze lingered on the house, one hand still on the door handle.

Finally, he said, "Maybe not wasted."

Casey frowned. "You really think he's connected?"

Will shook his head. "No. But Cain's reaching from inside those walls. If he's writing to Leary, he's writing to others."

The SUV's headlights cut through the dark as they pulled away, leaving the small house swallowed in shadow.

Will's jaw was tight, eyes on the windshield. "Cain wanted us to."

Casey turned. "You think he knew we'd land on Leary?"

"He circled the bait and left it where we'd find it. Visitor logs, fan mail, sermons, he knew we'd trip over Leary sooner or later."

"And while we're spinning our wheels, with basement dweller fan boy," Casey said grimly, "the body count climbs."

Will shifted the SUV into gear, his voice low. "That's Cain's game. He doesn't need to be out of his cell to waste our time. And Leary? He's just another piece off the board."

They pulled into the night, leaving Marcus Leary behind, a ghost of Cain's shadow, but nothing more.

Marcus stayed frozen on the basement stairs long after the SUV's taillights vanished through the blinds. His chest heaved. His mother's voice drifted down from the kitchen above.

"Marcus? You forgot your mail again."

He wiped sweat from his brow, forcing his voice steady. "What is it?"

She came down with a padded envelope in her hands, the return address scrawled in neat block letters. She smiled as if she were handing him a care package from camp.

"Your pen pal wrote again. Such a sweet boy, to keep in touch so regularly. Always right on time." She handed it over and patted his arm. "One day, I hope I get to meet him."

Marcus stared at the envelope, pulse pounding. The handwriting was familiar. The weight of it was heavier than paper had a right to be.

Julien Cain.

The letters came every two weeks, never late. The old monster had arranged it somehow — mail queued up like sermons on a schedule, arriving long after he was locked away.

His mother didn't know. To her, Cain was polite, respectful, almost charming on the page. She had no idea she was couriering poison into her own house.

Marcus clutched the envelope to his chest and whispered, "Teach me."

The Vicar Emerges

Kristen woke with a sharp gasp, the sheets twisted around her legs. Her heart was pounding so hard it blurred her vision. The dream was so vivid she could still hear his voice, Steve's laugh, deep and cold, echoing in the dark as if he stood right behind her.

She sat on the edge of the bed, rubbing her face. The house was quiet, but she could feel the memory clinging to her skin.

When Will came in from his early run, she didn't wait. "They're back," she said.

He paused in the doorway. "The nightmares?"

Kristen nodded, jaw clenched. "And it's always the same now, Steve, standing there, like he's... watching me. Laughing." She looked toward the window, as if searching for shadows. "I hate it because it feels like he knows something I don't."

Will crossed the room and rested a hand on her shoulder. "I'm telling you to go talk to someone, please, someone with an outside perspective. He's locked up. That laugh's just in your head."

Kristen didn't argue, but her eyes told him she wasn't convinced.

That afternoon, Will's phone buzzed with a secure message from Cybercrimes. The office was quiet as the video loaded. An encrypted file had surfaced on a fringe video forum, shaky, low-resolution footage, the frame swaying as if filmed by hand. Over it, a male voice spoke through heavy distortion:

"The fields are choked with weeds. The soil must be turned. The unworthy must be cut down."

The cadence was deliberate, almost liturgical, each phrase separated by a pause long enough to make the hair on Will's neck prickle.

It ended with a line that landed like a stone in the gut:

"Par is never enough."

Will and Casey watched it twice without saying a word.

"Great," Casey muttered. "Our killer's got a YouTube channel." She leaned back in her chair, arms crossed. "Half the country club is on Instagram, a guy could plan his whole round just scrolling."

Will's gaze stayed on the frozen final frame, the jagged waveform still pulsing at the bottom of the screen. "And now he's letting us know we're on the course with him."

Across town, Ellie and Emily were sitting on the family porch, scrolling their feeds.

"Oh, this is creepy," Ellie said, turning her phone so Emily could see. The same video, but stripped of the encryption watermark, played on her screen. "Some weirdo calling himself 'The Vicar'? Please. Sounds like a youth pastor trying to be scary."

Emily frowned. "Where'd you get that?"

"It's all over a message board I follow. Somebody must've ripped it from somewhere."

Ellie tapped the screen. "Check this line, *'Par is never enough.'* Total golf nerd edge-lord, right?"

Emily didn't reply. Her stomach tightened. This wasn't just creepy, it was fresh. Too fresh. She opened her phone and typed a message to her dad.

Public Sermon

Back at the precinct, Will tossed the tablet onto the table. "If Ellie's seeing that video, then so is half of Oakhaven. Which means the Vicar's either feeding it straight to the public, or someone close to him is doing the honors."

Casey crossed her arms and leaned against the edge of the table. "So what now—go public? Warn the targets?"

Will shook his head. "Keep quiet. Work the list. Don't spook him."

Casey's voice spiked. "So we give him a head start? We gamble with their lives?"

Will's reply was flat. "We'll see."

Casey leaned closer. "No, Will. That's not a strategy. That's giving him the pen to write the next obituary."

"And if we go public," Will countered, "we're daring him to escalate. This guy's not just keeping score, he's making a show of it. Give him a bigger audience and he'll play to it."

Silence stretched, thick with the weight of the choice.

Will rubbed his jaw, gaze fixed on the case board. Finally, he exhaled. "We go public. Controlled release, enough to get the word out without dumping the entire file. If he wants the spotlight, fine, we'll make sure it's blinding."

The press release went out just after 6 p.m., warning of "an ongoing investigation into multiple related homicides" and urging "those associated with the Rocky Pointe Country Club's former finance committee" to take precautions. No names. No specifics.

Three hours later, the Vicar posted again, this time directly to social media.

The video was sharper, the voice calmer but colder.

"The shepherds were warned. The sheep are restless. The flock will be thinned."

The camera panned slowly across a darkened room. In the corner, barely lit, sat a small table. On it: a folded golf scorecard in a clear evidence bag.

Casey's stomach sank. "That's—"

"Our scorecard," Will finished. His voice was low, clipped. "That was on my desk this morning."

The camera lingered on the bag for a heartbeat, then the distorted voice returned.

"Par is never enough."

The screen went black.

Casey looked at Will. "We've got a leak."

Will's jaw tightened. "Or a ghost walking our halls.

The Collector

The printer whirred in the dark, spitting out another sheet, this one a candid of Casey Murphy leaving the precinct, a coffee cup in hand, hair pulled back. The timestamp in the corner was three minutes old.

The man in the leather chair slid it into the growing folder marked "ANDERSON UNIT." Beneath it, other folders were already thick: WHITMORE, GILMORE, YATES. Each spine neat, each page numbered in his careful hand.

He tapped a pen against the margin of Casey's photo, jotting a single note: *Doubts herself. Watches others for cues. Easy to unbalance.*

Beside the folders sat a small wooden box. Inside, neatly arranged, were tokens. A silver cufflink dulled with age. A coffee mug with a faint lipstick ring etched into the rim. A child's hair clip, one tooth bent. Harmless things, ordinary things — but each stolen from homes whose locks had never stopped him.

His gaze lingered on the newest addition: a thin bracelet with a custom charm, the enamel still bright from being worn often. He let his finger trace the curve of the charm but didn't pick it up, as though touching it too long might dull the memory it carried.

She never even noticed I was there.

He closed the lid gently, almost reverently. The latch snapped shut with a soft finality.

Then he reached for a fresh file folder, the blank tab staring back. He wrote a single word in block letters: **ELLIE.**

Emily's Research

Emily sat cross-legged on her bedroom floor, laptop open beside her, highlighters scattered across the carpet like candy. Her criminology professor had assigned a project on criminal communication patterns, and she'd chosen The Vicar's sermons—partly because they fascinated her, partly because she hated not understanding the code.

The corkboard she'd pulled from Billy's room leaned against the wall. He hadn't needed it since transferring to UNC Chapel Hill. Billy had started at Ravenwood University, playing midfield on the men's lacrosse team while Julia played for the women's squad. They'd been inseparable—on the field, off it, bound up in the same circle of teammates and friends.

Then Julia was taken and ripped from her family, her life, her team. Everyone knew Julien Cain's hand was behind it; he was the one who touched her. His patterns, his "artwork," his influence had carved the wound. Her death had broken something in all of them, but in Billy it left a hollow so deep he couldn't bear to stay. Practices felt haunted, the locker rooms still carried her laugh, and every corner of Ravenwood whispered her absence. By mid-year, Billy had packed his gear and transferred to Chapel Hill, desperate to escape the shadows Cain had left behind.

Emily had carefully stacked his old playbooks and the photos of Julia from his wall before carrying the corkboard away. It felt wrong, like trespassing in a room that still belonged to both of them. She missed him more than she ever admitted out loud.

Now the board was already cluttered: sermon transcripts, scripture taped beside handwritten Roman numerals, photocopied scorecards from evidence stills, and Post-its linking verses to club events and dates. A thin red string stretched from a passage about "harvesting the fields" to a newspaper clipping about Oakhaven's charity tournament.

She scribbled a note — *Par = goal? Standard? Not enough?* — then stepped back, trying to see it through The Vicar's eyes.

The door opened without a knock.

"Emily." Kristen stood there, taking in the board in one slow sweep. "What is all this?"

"Class project," Emily said quickly. "It's for my criminal psych elective."

Kristen stepped inside, closing the door behind her. "This is case material."

Emily hesitated, then gestured to the board. "Some of it's public. The rest I pieced together... from transcripts, from what you and Dad talk about. Look—" She pointed to a printout from a news blog, a long-distance shot of the 18th green with police on scene. In the far corner, Kristen's silhouette was visible.

Kristen's gaze followed. "Probably a file photo from last year."

Emily shook her head firmly. "No. You wore that jacket last week."

Kristen's posture tightened. "That's exactly the problem," she said, voice low but sharp. "You're getting too close to something dangerous. This isn't schoolwork."

Emily straightened. "I'm just analyzing language. Words. Patterns. That's all."

Kristen's expression softened, but the tension in her shoulders didn't. "Words on paper are how he chooses victims." She reached up, plucked a Post-it off the board, and crumpled it. "Drop it, Emily. I don't want this spilling onto you."

From the hallway, a voice chimed in. "Ooooh, what's going on in here?"

Ellie leaned against the doorframe, earbuds looped around her neck, one hand still clutching her phone. Her eyes swept the corkboard with a grin. "Looks like you've got a full-on murder wall. CSI chic."

"It's not cool," Kristen snapped.

Ellie smirked. "Hey, I'm just saying—if you ever need help, Em, I can spot a shady TikTok account a mile away. Half my feed's true crime anyway."

Emily's glare cut across the room. "This isn't a game, Ellie. He's building a sequence." She tapped the scorecard with her pen. "These numbers aren't random."

Ellie lifted her hands in mock surrender. "Sure, Professor. Still looks like a murder Pinterest to me."

Kristen's eyes snapped to Ellie. Her voice was sharp. "Out."

Ellie backed away, grin intact. "Don't blame me when she cracks the case before you do."

Kristen turned back to Emily, softer now. "Promise me you'll drop this. For real."

Emily didn't answer.

Emily stood staring at the corkboard. The room was quiet now, except for Ellie drifting back in and flopping onto the bed. She chewed her gum, eyes flicking over the strings and scribbles.

Emily tapped the pinned scorecard with her pen, brow furrowed.

"It's structured like a round. Holes one through eighteen. But he isn't just playing golf, he's mapping people."

Ellie sprawled across the bed, gum snapping. "Or maybe he just sucks at counting. Five, six... whatever."

Emily didn't look up. She pointed to the red numerals she'd scrawled across a printout of the finance committee roster.

"V. Whitmore. VI. Gilmore. These aren't random bodies. They're strokes against the board. The first nine holes — I through IX — line up with the members who either stole or looked the other way."

She stepped back, eyes scanning the board. "Par is never enough. He's punishing them for indifference. For doing nothing."

Ellie sat up, chewing more slowly. "So we're not talking golf anymore. We're talking payback."

Emily underlined the numerals in her notebook. "No. We're talking judgment."

Drive-by Clue & Ellie's Leak

Casey was halfway up Whitmore's street when something caught her eye, a pinprick of color in the gutter, stark against the sheen of rain-slick concrete. She slowed, hazard lights blinking on the unmarked car, and stepped out into the damp air.

It was quiet here, the quiet you got in moneyed neighborhoods, no barking dogs, no humming AC units, just the faint hiss of rain sliding down leaves.

She crouched, using the edge of a pen to nudge the object free from a shallow puddle.

A golf tee. Blood-red, the lacquer dulled in spots, its head slightly nicked like it had seen real play. Near the base of the head, just below the chip, at the top of the shank, was a carving so small she almost missed it, a curling script **W** surrounded by a laurel wreath.

Casey stood upright, examining it beneath the streetlamp. "You won't find one of these at the pro shop," she said quietly, placing it into an evidence bag. Whoever had dropped it hadn't done so by accident. This was intentional, a detail meant to be noticed.

Later, in the lab, forensics backed up her suspicion. The material was hickory, solid, weighty, unlike the typical maple or birch found in factory-made tees. The red dye traced back to a niche supplier in Scotland known for crafting vintage-style golf accessories.

Years back, that same supplier had crafted materials for a special edition club set, a small batch made exclusively for the Rocky Pointe Country Club's finance committee.

Whitmore's name had been among the recipients. Casey was still mulling that over when she rang Will.

"You're not going to like this," she told him. "I'm already not liking most of what I'm hearing lately,"

Will said. "What've you got?"

She laid it out, the hickory wood, the Scottish supplier, the tie to the finance committee. There was a long silence, just enough for her to notice the quiet settle on his end.

"Finance committee," he said at last. "Whitmore, Gilmore..." His tone turned sharp. "They're all either dead or next on our list."

"Exactly." "You think the killer just dropped it?" Will asked.

Casey looked back at the gutter where she'd found it, the rain still curling lazily in circles. "Dropped? No. He left it there on purpose. He wanted it seen."

Another beat passed. When Will spoke again, his voice was quiet. "Then he's not just playing through," he told her. "He's setting the course."

Back at the Office

Will was nudging a case file toward the edge of his desk when the Cybercrimes alert pinged: **New Upload - Encrypted Sermon Video.**

He clicked it open.

The Vicar's warped voice seeped through the speakers as shaky, handheld footage played, as if filmed from the shadows. Moonlight spilled across the edge of a golf course, the flag whipping in the wind, damp grass catching the light in sharp flashes. The sermon's rhythm was jarring, broken by uneven pauses, like scripture twisted out of shape:

"The righteous shall inherit the earth... but the corrupt shall be cut down where they stand."

The camera shifted, zeroing in on a sheet of paper pinned to a rough wooden wall. The shot held steady.

Thick black handwriting covered the page, a list of names, some underlined, others encircled with firm, purposeful strokes. Will's eyes fixed on one name near the center.

James R. Calloway.

The name hit hard, not because Calloway was unfamiliar, but because that name appeared in only one place beyond Will's memory: Emily's corkboard upstairs in her bedroom.

And now, it had surfaced in The Vicar's video. Casey glanced from the monitor to Will. "You're thinking it's   family?"

"I'm thinking I need to go look for myself."

Will stood there a long moment, the glow from the monitor fading into the muted hum of the precinct. His reflection stared back from the black screen — tired eyes, jaw tight, the faint ache behind them that came from too many late nights staring at ghosts.

He was reaching for his coat when the desk phone rang — sharp, slicing through the quiet.

He hesitated before answering. "Anderson."

The voice on the other end was low, strained but steady. "Detective. It's Graham Holloway."

Will straightened. "You don't usually call me direct."

"Yeah, well," Holloway said, his tone rough around the edges, "something tells me the clock's running out. We should talk. Off the record."

Will's hand tightened on the receiver. "You know something about the video?"

"I know what's missing from it," Holloway said. A faint sound of movement — maybe a coffee cup set down. "Meet me at the Harbor Diner. Back booth. Bring that moral compass of yours."

The line went dead.

Will stared at the receiver for a second longer, then hung up. The unease in Holloway's voice wasn't fear — it was confession waiting to happen.

He grabbed his coat. "I'll see for myself," he muttered again, though now the direction had changed.

Across town, Will slid into the booth without waiting for an invitation.

Across from him, Graham Holloway barely looked up from his coffee. The mug was half-empty, black and cooling, but he held it like something ceremonial.

"Thought you might ghost me," Holloway said, eyes still fixed on the window. "You're not the off-the-record type."

Will set his hands on the table. "You said you had something for me."

Holloway reached into his jacket pocket and pulled out a small plastic bag. Inside was a single red golf tee — hickory, lacquered, marked with a faded Roman numeral: IX.

"I found this last week," Holloway said quietly, sliding it across the table. "Top shelf in my locker. No note. Just sitting there like it had been waiting."

Will turned the bag over once in his hand, studying it. "You didn't report it."

"Didn't think it was a message for the department," Holloway said. He took a slow sip. "Thought it was personal."

Will's eyes flicked to the tee again. "Why would the killer leave you one?"

Another pause. This one heavier.

"Maybe because I was in the room when it all got built," Holloway said. "The votes. The silence. The way Whitmore steered people without leaving fingerprints."

Will's jaw tensed. "You signed off on the April 14th transfer — the one that funded Steve's front company."

"I signed a lot of things, Anderson." Holloway's eyes flicked toward him. "Some of them I shouldn't have. But you know how it works. A few lines buried in a packet, a late-night vote, and everyone's too tired or too greedy to read the fine print."

"You benefited."

"Yes," Holloway said, without hesitation.

Will leaned in. "So why aren't you dead yet?"

Holloway's laugh was low, humorless. "Because I didn't pretend I was clean. The others — Gilmore, Whitmore — they wore their sins like silk ties. I kept mine close to the skin."

"That sounds like a confession."

"That sounds like survival."

Will sat back, watching him. The bagged tee rested between them like a final warning.

"I always thought you knew more than you let on," Will said. "But I could never prove it."

"You weren't wrong."

Another beat.

"And now?" Will asked.

"Now," Holloway said, folding his hands around the mug, "I'm just a loose end. But I think the Vicar wants me to stay that way. For now."

Will rose, sliding the evidence bag off the table. "He's not done. And if he comes for you—"

"Then I'll deserve whatever number he gives me."

Will paused. Holloway's reflection in the window looked older, smaller, like a man already halfway gone.

Behind him, Holloway said, "Be careful, Anderson. He's not just hunting the guilty. He's watching the ones who look away."

Will didn't respond. Just pushed the door open and walked out into the dusk, the red tee rattling softly in the bag like a warning that hadn't landed. Not yet.

Anderson House – Upstairs

Emily's bedroom door stood ajar, with lamplight casting a warm glow into the hallway. Inside, her corkboard dominated the wall above the desk, covered in sermon clippings, Roman numerals, copied scorecards, and the names of victims, all neatly pinned in rows.

Ellie was perched cross-legged on the bed, scrolling through her phone. "So... my post kind of blew up," she said, flashing a grin.

Emily walked in from the bathroom, wrapped in a towel, brushing out her damp hair. "What post?"

Ellie turned her phone to show her. A screenshot of the corkboard filled the screen, close-ups of handwritten notes, red thread, and victim names, with the caption: Guess I'm a detective now.

Emily's eyes widened. "You posted that?"

"It's friends-only," Ellie replied with a casual shrug. "It's not like The Vicar is creeping through my feed."

Emily felt a twist in her gut. "Ellie... one of those names wasn't public."

Ellie's smile faded into a frown. "So? No one knows what it means."

Emily hesitated, then opened her own social app. "Did you watch the new video yet?"

Ellie tapped play. The distorted voice echoed from the phone's speaker. The camera zoomed in on the same name on the board.

"Oh..." Ellie's grin disappeared.

"I saw that site you were on. That support group thing."

Emily didn't look up from her corkboard. "And?"

"Some of those girls," Ellie said, lowering her voice, "they were upper-class when we were freshmen. Now they're at Ravenwood. The stuff they wrote—blackouts, waking up back in their rooms, clothes changed—" She stopped, uneasy. "It sounded like what Mom said Steve used to do."

Emily pressed a pin into the board, sharp and final. "Then it's not just stories. It's still happening. You have to be careful,"

"You think I don't get it? I've read everything he's ever posted. The way he talks? He's begging for attention. So I gave him some," Ellie snapped. "Better me than Mom. Better me than you. I just wanted to be cool."

Kitchen – Moments Later

Will stepped in through the back door, coat still on. Kristen stood at the counter, flipping through the mail. She saw his face and immediately set the stack aside. "What happened?"

He placed his phone on the counter, the video frozen on a name displayed in white over black. "That was never in a press release. Never in a shared file. The only place it existed outside my head..." He gestured toward the stairs. "...was on Emily's corkboard."

Kristen's brow creased. "You think Emily—?"

"Either that or this guy was in our house and took the photo himself. I think someone saw it," Will said. "Which means logically, the leak isn't in the department. It's in our home. With all the security upgrades after our last ordeal, I doubt someone was in here."

From upstairs, the quiet sound of the girls talking floated down. Kristen's phone buzzed with a social media notification. The preview showed Ellie's profile picture next to a caption: Guess the club's got more secrets than a confession booth.

Will's jaw tightened. "If he's quoting what's on our walls, Kristen... we're already playing his game."

"And before you ask," Will added tightly, "Casey remotely checked the security footage. No break-ins, no motion triggers, nothing physical. If someone saw that board, they either piggybacked our Wi-Fi or got it through a social feed."

Will's hand was already on the banister, his voice sharp and curt. "Girls, down here. Now."

Footsteps pounded on the stairs before Emily and Ellie appeared, Emily clutching a notebook to her chest.

Ellie trailed behind, trying to seem casual, but the tension in her face betrayed her nerves.

Kristen crossed her arms, her tone calm but firm. "Who wants to explain how something from Emily's board ended up in a Vicar video?"

Emily's eyes went wide. "What? No, wait, I never—"

She turned to her sister. "Ellie."

Ellie winced, then raised her chin. "It wasn't like that. I just... I thought her project looked real.

Like a legit murder board, you know?

She's been super into it—pulling stuff together, writing notes, adding string and all. It looked smart. Like something the FBI would do."

Will's stare cut through her. "So you took a picture of it."

Ellie hugged herself so tightly her shoulders hunched, nails digging into her own arms. The words tumbled out, brittle and fast.

"Yeah, but I didn't post it for everyone. It was just my private group—friends only. Just us. I never thought it would leak."

Kristen stepped in, her shadow cutting across the counter, voice rising like a whipcrack. "Ellie, you can't control screenshots! One person shares it, and it's gone. Forever." She stabbed a finger toward the glowing phone between them.

"How many times have I told you? Never send compromising pictures of yourself, never hand over leverage. This is the same damn thing."

Ellie flinched. Her lip trembled, and her eyes darted anywhere but her mother's—walls, floor, the fridge hum in the corner—like she could hide inside the kitchen itself. Her fingers twisted the hem of her hoodie until the fabric bunched in knots. "I didn't think it mattered," she whispered. "The names didn't mean anything—it was just a joke, an inside thing." Her throat tightened, tears breaking loose as the last words cracked out. "I didn't think... I didn't think anyone else would ever see it."

Will's jaw tensed, his voice dropping. "Well, someone did. And now your name, your sister's notes, and our home are in a killer's sermon. He's not just somewhere out there—he's in here."

Emily clutched her notebook tighter, guilt flooding her expression. "I told you not to mess with it," she whispered, staring at Ellie.

Ellie's bravado crumbled. She blinked quickly, trying not to cry. "I just wanted to matter, okay?" Ellie's voice cracked. "You're the smart one. The detective. I'm just... noise."

The room fell silent. Kristen's face softened, but the fear didn't fade from her eyes.

"You are not useless," she said fiercely. "But you are reckless. And right now, recklessness could get someone killed."

Will finally leaned in, both hands planted on the counter, eyes locked on the girls.

His tone was calm, but hard as steel. "You think it's just posts and likes, but there are people who live in the wires. The ones Steve worked with, they're still out there. And they don't need to step foot in this house to see inside it. No more posts. No more photos. No more games. From now on, what happens in this house stays in this house. Understood?"

The twins glanced at each other—Ellie's face flushed, Emily's eyes glossy—but both nodded.

Will let the silence linger another second. Then he pushed the phone across the counter. The Vicar's video frozen on the screen. "Because this—this is what a mistake costs. And I won't let it be yours."

Upstairs – Emily's Room

The tension downstairs still clung to them as Emily shut her bedroom door with a soft click. Ellie sank onto the edge of the bed. The silence stretched, broken only by the faint hum of the house settling.

Emily crossed her arms, pacing once before she turned on her twin. Her voice cracked with frustration. "Why Emily folded her arms, pacing once before coming to a stop. "Why would you do that? You knew better. You knew he'd see it if it got out."

Ellie hunched, twisting the hem of her shirt. "Because I didn't think I mattered, Em. You had the board, the notes, Mom's attention, and Dad's trust. And me? I'm the one who mouths off. The dumb one." Her voice broke. "I just wanted to show I could see things too."

Emily froze, her anger softening.

Ellie finally looked up, tears bright. "I just wanted to be... like you."

Hole of Judgment

A second video surfaced less than two hours after Ellie's photo leaked. No tags. No caption. Just the same warped watermark and a low-res title:

"Sermon: The Hole of Judgment."

The camera opened on a stone tee box, empty, wind scattering blades of grass across the slab. At its center lay an old Bible, splayed open and rain-soaked, pages fluttering like broken wings.

The Vicar's voice rolled out low and distorted, steady as liturgy:

"They built altars in boardrooms."

"They baptized greed in the name of charity."
"They smiled for the cameras."

"But the flock was never theirs to lead."

The lens shifted, unsteady. For a heartbeat, the camera revealed a wall lined with golf tees, each carved with Roman numerals, arranged in rows like offerings to a god.

"The hole is not a place of triumph."

"It is a grave."

The frame wavered again, rising shakily through mist, until the shot locked on a two-story home barely visible through the trees—the Anderson house.

Will's chest went rigid. Beside him, Casey leaned forward, eyes narrowing to slits.

The voice returned, closer now, almost intimate:

"Each stroke is a judgment."

"Each number, a truth revealed."

"The glove does not forget."

A pause, deliberate and heavy.

"The green knows who watched... and said nothing."

And then, soft as a benediction:

"Par is never enough."

The screen cut to black. No sender. No trace. Just the certainty that someone had stood close, close enough to point a camera at their home.

Message in the Fog

Fog rolled in early over Rocky Pointe. Thick and low, it curled over the fairways like smoke, turning manicured greens into ghost-country. Visibility was maybe twenty yards, and that was being generous. Floodlights from the cart barn behind the 12th hole did little more than make the mist glow from inside, as if it were alive.

Brent Harker hated mornings like this. He liked things clear — dirt, dew, divots. Fog screwed with depth perception, and worse, it made sounds lie. Every rustle of leaves became something slinking closer.

He muttered to himself as he walked the edge of the 13th fairway, lugging a garbage pail and a rake. The dawn crew was supposed to spread out across zones, but his radio crackled dead. He figured the others were holed up in the shed, waiting for the fog to lift.

Cowards.

He jabbed the rake into the rough, working the edge of the sand trap. That's when the teeth caught on something square. Not root, not stone. Compact.

"Dammit."

He crouched, fingers digging through damp soil, and pulled free a small leather-bound book: black leather, red-edged pages. Warped at the corners, but the spine pristine. He flipped it open.

A Bible.

Not new, but cared for. Revelation was underlined in red, margins crawling with tight script. What made his stomach clench was the inside cover: three letters, thick in flaking red ink.

V.M.C.

The "M" hooked downward, like a scythe.

Harker glanced around. Nothing but fog and silence.

Curiosity won. He flipped to the last page of Revelation, Chapter 22. Red pen slashed through verses:

"Let him who is unjust be unjust still... behold, I come quickly; and my reward is with me."

Below it, again: **V.M.C.**

And beneath that: *"13:13 — Mark of the Beast / Mark of the Bystander."*

Thirteen thirteen. The hole number? Or a time?

A branch cracked in the trees. Deliberate.

"Who's there?" Harker barked.

No answer. The fog swallowed sound like water.

By the time he reached the cart barn, the Bible was zipped inside his windbreaker. He wasn't superstitious, but nine years on this course taught him what didn't belong.

And this Bible didn't belong.

Oakhaven PD – Bullpen

Will was halfway through a stale witness statement when a knock came. Too light for Casey, too late for a social call.

Brent Harker stood in the doorway, grounds uniform damp with fog, clutching the Bible like it might squirm free.

"Detective Anderson?"

Will frowned. "Brent, right? Morning crew."

"Yeah. Look, I wasn't gonna say anything — figured it was some nut leaving religious junk. But after those videos, after Gilmore..."

Will stood. "What did you find?"

Harker stepped forward and laid the Bible on the desk, gentle as glass. The leather was slick, seams still damp. Will opened it carefully. Verses cut through Revelation in angry red. Then the initials.

V.M.C.

"It was buried shallow, off the 13th trap," Harker said. "Wrapped in cloth. Not random."

Will flipped to the back, scanning the scrawl: *"13:13 — Mark of the Beast / Mark of the Bystander."*

The handwriting was the same as the Vicar's overlays.

"This is him," Will murmured.

Harker shifted uneasily. "Think he's planning something at the 13th?"

Will's thumb traced the ink. *Mark of the Bystander.* His chest tightened.

"I think he already did."

PD Evidence Room – Evening

Fluorescents buzzed overhead, their stuttery rhythm clawing at Casey's nerves. She set a coffee beside Will.

"You texted me a 911 Bible-nerd emergency. Either you joined a cult, or we've got something new."

Will didn't look up. He tapped the initials bleeding across the inside cover. "V.M.C. And here—'13:13. Mark of the Beast. Mark of the Bystander.'"

Casey pulled on gloves and flipped through the pages carefully. Red ink underlined Revelation in jagged streaks. Margins filled with tight script bled into the text, twisting it.

She frowned, tracing the initials with a fingertip. "V.M.C... not a book of the Bible. Not Latin I recognize. Could be code. Or..." She tilted the book toward the light. "Vicar of... something. Vicar of Man's... Condemnation? Correction?"

Will's gaze sharpened, but he stayed silent as she read aloud:

"I am he which searcheth the hearts..." She turned a page. "Who is like unto the beast? Who can make war with him?" Another. "They have no rest, day nor night..."

Casey exhaled slowly, setting the Bible flat. "This isn't an obsession. It's a manifesto. And if V.M.C. is a signature, then it's not just initials. It's a title. *The Vicar of Mortal Correction.*"

Will's jaw tightened. He turned a page to find Revelation 17:6, underlined so hard it tore the paper. The woman drunk with the blood of the saints. In the margin, a scrawl: K.A.

His chest tightened. "Kristen's initials."

Casey froze, her voice low. "He's not just quoting scripture. He's assigning it. Warping their verses, their lives. V.M.C.–the Vicar's claiming authority, like some twisted ecclesiastical stamp."

Will nodded grimly. "Marking them twice. In the Bible. On the course."

Casey flipped again–and stopped cold. A faint pencil sketch ghosted between the pages. Female. Hollow eyes. A cheer jacket.

"That's Ellie," she whispered.

Will's reply was raw, immediate. "She's not a symbol. She's prophecy he's trying to write."

The Bible lay between them, half-Scripture, half-madness.

Casey leaned back, her voice sharp with unease. "This is religion as stalking. Theology as blueprint. And now initials as a creed."

Will met her eyes, steady but dark. "He's not killing out of chaos. He's killing to correct."

She frowned. "Correct what?"

Will turned to Revelation 3:16, underlined twice, the margin marked with block letters: Because you are lukewarm... I will spit you out.

He closed the book with a flat snap. "Indifference."

Anderson Home – Late Night (Kristen's Office)
Rain tapped the windows like fingers too patient to be ignored. Kristen nursed a second glass of Jameson, the

Bible on her desk atop an evidence bag Will had left behind. His notes on the legal pad that accompanied it.

She opened it. Revelation 17:3–4: *The woman on the scarlet beast... golden cup of abominations...*

The Whore of Babylon.

Beside it, in tight script: *False virtue is the deadliest mask. A judge who sleeps beside evil cannot claim innocence. K.A.*

Her initials.

Kristen's hand clenched. This wasn't about her DA role. It was about Steve. About silence. About the predator she'd let into her house.

Another page: *No mother is blameless.*

Her eyes lingered on the scrawl. A part of her wanted to flip through every page, to see if other initials waited. Her daughters' initials. But she couldn't. Not yet. She closed the Bible instead, convincing herself there would be nothing there. Denial was safer.

The chair scraped as she shot to her feet, glass shaking in her grip. In the kitchen window, her reflection looked like someone else. Too many secrets.

Will's voice came from the doorway. "You read it."

"He knows what I was. What I let happen."

Will stepped closer, steady. "He twisted Scripture to sound like justice. But he's wrong."

Kristen shook her head. "Don't give me absolution. I didn't survive. I coexisted. And because of that, Emily got hurt. I let a monster touch their lives. Touch me."

Her voice hardened. "He's right about one thing. I know who deserves punishment. I just never thought I'd be one of them."

Silence stretched.

Finally, she turned, jaw locked. "If he comes after them again, I won't wait for the law."

Will didn't flinch. "Neither will I."

Anderson Attic – Late Night

The attic smelled of old quilts and rosewater perfume. Emily curled beneath a beam, the Bible on her knees. She'd overheard her parents arguing. She needed to see for herself.

Page 595. Daniel 3:27.

The fire had no power... nor was a hair singed...

Beside it, the date of her assault.

Her throat tightened. A brittle laugh escaped. Fire had no power? A lie. The fire marked her every time a door clicked, every time someone called her "mature."

In the margin, new words: *The unmarked suffer in silence. The next generation of rot. E.A.*

Her initials.

Her pulse stayed steady. He thought silence meant weakness. He thought she was rot.

He didn't understand her at all.

Emily set the Bible aside and wrote in her notebook: **"Daniel 3:27."** She underlined it.

"Okay," she whispered into the dark. "You want me in the story? I'm in."

Emily's Room – After Midnight

The house was quiet. Ellie snored down the hall.

Emily scrolled her private feed. Buried in her DMs:

From: *BookofNumbersV6*

Daniel 3:27. Fire does not leave scars. Prove you belong among the pure.

Her skin prickled. She typed back: *Fire refines gold.*

The message was read.

A long pause.

Her hand trembled, hovering over the keys. She almost deleted it. Almost.

Then came the reply: *Then show me your gold.*

Her fear shifted into something sharper. She flipped to a clean page of her notebook.

Phase One: Earn His Trust.

No Mulligans

The livestream was low quality, but clear enough to see a woman tied to a chair, a golf glove covering her mouth, her head drooping like a forgotten doll.

The light flickered, then held steady, exposing the corrugated metal walls around her. In the corner, something shiny caught the camera's eye, the chrome sheen of golf clubs packed into a bag.

"Maintenance shed," Casey said, already moving, her voice sharp and confident.

Will pulled his vest from the back of his chair. "North side or south?"

"North," she replied, chambering a round into her rifle. "Closest one by the fence line."

Minutes later, SWAT stacked up at the outbuilding's door. No need to knock and announce; extenuating circumstances override the search warrant requirement, as this was a matter of life or death. The ram struck twice —boom, boom —before the lock screeched and gave way. The door banged open. The stack disappeared like water going into a drain.

The "victim" inside turned out to be nothing but a mannequin, a cheap female form with a wig slipping loose, wrists bound to a folding chair with zip ties. A golf glove was taped over the plastic face.

In the corner, the livestream camera kept running, its tiny red light throbbing like a heartbeat.

Casey froze in the doorway, her jaw clenched. "Son of a—" She cut herself short, sweeping the shadows with her eyes. Nothing. No footprints in the thin layer of dust. No trace of sweat, perfume, or presence. Whoever set this up hadn't lingered a second longer than necessary.

"Well, technically, this may be a crime scene; we need to get the CSU gang in here," Casey said to Will. "Somebody call Command and have them send a team. And maybe a Jedi while we're at it—because whoever pulled this off didn't leave a single damn footprint."

One of the tac radios crackled. "Unit Bravo-Twelve from Command, we've got a report of another scene. Ravenwood University chapel. Notify the Detectives to respond."

Casey looked to Will. "It's him. He's already moving while we're stuck here."

By the time they were back in the car, pulling off their vests, the sirens had gone silent, halfway to the next scene.

The chapel's stained-glass windows threw fractured pools of moonlight across the pews. Dust hung in the air, clinging to the scent of old incense. The silence was so deep their footsteps echoed as if the walls disapproved.

On the steps of the altar sat Victoria Yates. Her body had been posed in grotesque reverence, head bowed, hands loose in her lap, skirt smoothed across her knees. In the dim light, she could have been praying—until the wet black Roman numeral painted across her skirt broke the illusion: *IV.*

Casey crouched near the body, her jaw set. The paint's odor was sharp, chemical, freshly biting at the air. *Deliberate. Controlled. Staged.*

And then she saw the rest.

A trail of condoms was scattered down the stone steps, aligned like markers leading away from the altar. Each wrapper caught a glint of colored light through the stained glass. At the trail's end, half in shadow, lay Yates's underwear—folded neatly, disturbingly intimate. Resting on top was a Rocky Pointe Golf Club scorecard.

The crest gleamed in the light: a flagstick, crossed irons, a pale shimmer of a lake. A brand, not just a logo. Here, in the chapel, it looked less like membership and more like ownership.

Casey turned the card over with a gloved hand. Red letters bled into the back:

SCORECARD FULL, BODY EMPTY.

Will stood rigid, gaze fixed on the words. Yates wasn't random. She'd once sat on the finance committee, tied to the same toxic scandal as Whitmore and Gilmore. The Roman numeral fit the pattern. But the condoms, the underwear, the posture of prayer—this wasn't just scorekeeping. It was *humiliation.* Sexual shame weaponized.

His chest tightened. This felt closer to Steve's world, to Cain's: trafficking, silence, shame. *The Vicar wasn't just* punishing corruption. *He was desecrating reputations, turning their secrets inside out.*

Casey broke the silence. "Seriously? Roman numerals, golf, Bible verses? It's like Palpatine and Tiger Woods had a lovechild."

Will glanced at her, grim. "That's a disturbing thought."

Casey allowed herself a thin grin. "You're welcome."

Her eyes swept the altar again. Across the rail, black block letters scarred the wood:

THE HARVEST IS PLENTIFUL, BUT THE WORKERS ARE FEW.

Casey exhaled hard. "He had us chasing shadows while he made his move."

Will's gaze followed the scripture upward. The Good Shepherd stared back through cracked glass, light slicing across his face until it looked skeletal. His skin prickled. This wasn't just scripture twisted for effect. It was *recruitment.* A sermon master looking for disciples.

"No," he said quietly. "He had us exactly where he wanted us."

Casey's frustration cut sharply in the silence. "What does all this mean? This guy is frustrating me to no end—cryptic crap, like he's running a damn Bible study in hell."

Will didn't answer. His focus had shifted to a detail sharper than scripture. The perfume. Faint, but familiar. He'd smelled it in the clubhouse corridor, clinging to one of the staff. A woman. Not the Vicar's style. Not his ritual. *Something else is bleeding into the scene.*

His phone buzzed, the vibration loud in the silence. DHS Rivers. A single message:

Clubhouse employee Gregory Young may have offshore ties. Restaurant staff. Worth questioning. Will update if I get more.

Will's thumb hovered above the screen. His eyes flicked from the painted IV on Yates's skirt to the condoms on the steps. *A woman's perfume in a crime staged like this. Not from Yates.*

"There's someone else in this," he muttered. "And she was here."

That afternoon, Ellie pulled her hair back into a high ponytail. She laced up her black-and-white Nike Pegasus shoes, not her usual bold, bright blue men's Hoka Mach X2s. She always said men's shoes had better options.

She slipped into her usual trail gear: a slate-gray Lululemon Swiftly Tech tank and deep teal Hotty Hot low-rise shorts, which draped loosely around her thighs. The built-in liner, when her shorts occasionally caught the breeze, peeked through. A black running belt circled her hips, with a small zippered pouch clipped on. She didn't run to draw attention. She ran to enjoy the outdoors. It was the same outfit she wore on nearly every run.

Rain or shine, summer or winter, she was easily recognizable on the trails.

That evening, the setting sun turned the fairways into liquid gold. Pine tree shadows stretched long and thin. At the overlook by the 12th hole, she stopped briefly.

She held her phone at arm's length and snapped a quick selfie.

Sunglasses on. Half a smirk on her face. The pristine green lay neatly behind her.

By dinner time, the photo was on her private feed.

Guess I'm in the fancy part of town.

Later, Kristen sat at the dining table. Her sleeves were rolled up. She was knee-deep in court briefs.

Her phone buzzed—no caller ID.

Just a single photo with a message:

Hole 12's not her best side.

Her stomach clenched.

Meanwhile, at the Precinct

Will and Casey scanned video from outside Ravenwood Chapel at the time of the murder.

Casey's hand froze on the keyboard. "Hold up." She tapped the screen. "Tell me that doesn't look familiar."

As the killer slinks out of frame, a shadowy figure stops and looks in a different direction.

In the corner of the image, beyond the broken stained glass, was a figure in profile from the adjacent golf course.

A high ponytail. Sleeveless top. Shorts that reflected the light differently at the hem. A black band around the waist.

Will grabbed his phone. He opened Ellie's 12th-hole selfie. He placed it side by side with the still.

It wasn't just familiar. It was identical. Right down to the white swoosh on the shoes.

And the teal flash beneath the shorts.

"She wasn't alone out there," Will said, lowering his voice.

Casey's jaw set. "And whoever it was? She knew her. Could've called her by name."

Will's phone buzzed, Kristen's name flashing across the screen. The second he answered, her voice came ragged, pitched with panic.

"Will—someone just sent me a photo of Ellie. On the golf course. It came from an unknown number."

His stomach dropped. "Where is she now? Is she inside? Did she come in from her run?"

"Yes—she just got home. Five minutes ago. She's upstairs in the shower."

He was already moving, keys in hand. "Lock the doors. Every window, too. Don't wait—do it now. I'm on my way."

Kristen's heart hammered as she hung up. The cheerful hiss of the shower upstairs made her chest tighten—Ellie humming to herself, blissfully unaware.

She darted to the back door first, sliding the deadbolt into place. The kitchen window was cracked open an inch; she slammed it shut, hands trembling as the frame rattled. In the reflection on the glass, she saw only her own wide eyes, but her pulse told her someone could be standing just beyond the trees, watching.

Living room—locked. Dining room—locked. She forced herself down the hall, barefoot on the hardwood, every board creaking louder than she remembered. She checked the front door twice, then three times, jiggling the handle until she was sure.

A muffled thud overhead—just the shower caddy tipping, she told herself. Just Ellie moving. But the sound sent her racing for the staircase anyway, her breath shallow.

"Ellie?" she called up, hating the thin edge of her own voice. No answer, only the rush of water.

Kristen pressed a palm to the banister to steady herself. She wanted to run upstairs, to drag her daughter out dripping and confused, but Will's voice echoed in her head: *Lock everything. Stay calm. Don't let them see you panic.*

She forced herself to turn toward the study instead. The last window. The one that never quite latched. She shoved it down, locked it, and pulled the curtains tight.

Only then did she notice the glow on her phone, still in her other hand—the photo staring back at her. Ellie was caught mid-stride on the golf course path, the sun cutting across her face. A perfect shot. Too close.

Kristen's throat went dry. Whoever had taken it hadn't used a zoom lens from the tree line.

They'd been standing right there.

Anderson House – Upstairs

Kristen didn't wait; she walked into the bathroom and pulled back the shower curtain. Kristen's hand was trembling as she held up her phone. "What the hell, Mom?" Ellie shrieked.

The photo filled the screen, Ellie, mid-stride on the fairway, her ponytail caught in motion, her black running belt glinting under the sun. The shot was angled from behind, zoomed so tight it traced her from head to toe.

Ellie froze, water still bearing down on her hair from the shower. "That's me," she whispered, voice thin. "That's literally from this afternoon."

Kristen's voice cracked, fear bleeding into anger. "He was *right there*, Ellie. Feet from you. Close enough to hear you breathe. He sent this to me. Do you understand what that means?"

Ellie's mouth opened, then shut again. She looked at the picture and shook her head slowly. "That's just... my route. The trail cuts near the twelfth fairway. I didn't know, I had no clue anyone was even there." She turned off the water and grabbed the towel that Kristen had picked up from the counter.

The garage door opened and shut, and then Will walked in.

"Kristen, Ellie, Emily?" he sounded out.

"Upstairs." Kristen calls out, "She's getting out of the shower and dressed, be right down."

As Kristen and Ellie came down the stairs, Will raised his head and stepped forward, jaw clenched, his voice laced with the commanding tone Ellie usually hated.

"He wasn't just there. He saw you. He chose you. And he wanted your mother to know it." He pointed sharply at the photo. "That's not some random shot. That's a warning."

Ellie swallowed hard, her bravado stripped away. "I didn't— I swear, I didn't know. I was just running."

Will says, "I saw him on the security video from campus stop and look at you mere moments after he left another victim in the university's chapel."

Kristen turned, leaning in front of her daughter so they were eye level. Her voice was low but fierce. "You don't run alone again. Not through the course, not around the lake, not down the damn street. You don't step out of this house without your sister or an adult. Do you hear me?"

Ellie's eyes filled, a rare flicker of shame breaking through. "Mom—"

"No, Ellie." Kristen's hand gripped her daughter's knee, hard enough to anchor her. "He *sent me your picture.* He could have taken you. He wanted me to *see* that." Her voice trembled. "Do you have any idea what that feels like?"

Ellie's lips pressed tight, the words stuck behind her throat. She nodded once, small and stiff.

Will's gaze softened, but only slightly. "This isn't just about rules, El. This is survival. From here on, you move as a team. No exceptions."

Emily appeared in the doorway, wide-eyed, glancing between her sister and the phone. For once, Ellie didn't argue. She just crossed her arms around herself and whispered, "Okay."

Emily decided right then that she was done. No more taunting, no more replies. What had started as some creepy online game had crossed a line; it wasn't personal anymore. It was dangerous.

Kristen exhaled shakily, lowering the phone at last. The image still burned in her mind, her daughter's outline, unaware, oblivious, a target framed through a predator's lens.

For the first time, Ellie seemed to feel it too.

Club's Dirty History

The library's microfilm reader hummed softly as Casey scrolled through decades-old editions of the *Oakhaven Gazette*. Headlines flickered past, golf tournaments, ribbon cuttings, alumni luncheons, until a smaller article caught her eye.

CLUB, RAVENWOOD PARTNER FOR ENVIRONMENTAL CLEANUP

Except the subhead told another story: *State Probe Into Alleged Waste Dumping Dropped.*

"Here," Casey said, tapping the screen. The article detailed complaints from residents about strange runoff near the old quarry, whispers of toxic disposal, and a sudden withdrawal of the investigation after "private remediation funds" were offered.

Will leaned closer. "Private remediation from the golf club."

"And the university's endowment," Casey added.

She kept scrolling, and a grainy black-and-white photo filled the frame, a charity gala from the same year. In the front row, beaming for the camera, stood a younger Kristen Anderson beside Emily, maybe twelve years old, in a dress two sizes too big. The caption listed Kristen as an event co-chair.

Casey smirked faintly. "You Andersons are a public-facing bunch. If someone wanted to study you, your habits, your schedule, they could build a scrapbook from the society pages alone."

Will's jaw tightened, but he didn't argue.

Casey started pulling other clippings. One by one, a pattern emerged: every victim they'd ID'd so far had ties to the cover-up, a board member, a contractor, a university trustee.

Holloway Remembers

Holloway stood by the trophy case, one hand absently tracing Whitmore's engraved name, the glass cool beneath his fingers. He remembered the meeting like it was yesterday, back when the finance committee still met behind the wine cellar, away from nosy servers and nosier spouses.

"The golf course is just a front," Whitmore had said, swirling his scotch. "What matters is the land beneath it. The south ridge, the wetland zoning, the undeclared lot behind the marina—that's the real asset."

Graham had watched the others nod; Gilmore chuckled, their silence was paid for with favors, false invoices, and board votes disguised as 'maintenance funding.'

They'd shuffled funds through the Ravenwood Development Trust, routed through shell firms with names like GreenEdge Holdings and Fairway Futures. They weren't laundering money. They were sterilizing it, turning bloodied investment cash into clean equity.

Whitmore had closed that meeting with a smirk. "No one looks at us. Not here. Country clubs are built on secrets. Just make sure no one digs deep enough to find the foundation."

Holloway stepped away from the case now, but the words still echoed. Secrets buried under soil, old greens, and a land grab that was supposed to stay buried. Until the Vicar started unearthing them one corpse at a time.

Will checks in with Kristen

Will calls Kristen and runs the information by her about what they just found, asking if any of it came up in the corruption investigation. He tells her they found two suspicious-looking women at a charity gala from about four years ago. "Want to explain where you were that night, madam DA?" Kristen laughs and responds, "If you had been there, then you wouldn't have to ask."

"Okay, okay, point taken, I'm hanging up now," Will says.

Across the room, Ellie padded in barefoot, earbuds slung around her neck. She lingered by the doorway, pretending to scroll through her phone while Kristen and Will discussed the names in low voices.

A few minutes later, upstairs in her room, Ellie typed the list into a search bar. Halfway down the page, she stopped. One name, Robert Albright, came with a photo she recognized instantly.

Her friend's grandfather.

She stared at the screen for a long moment, thumb hovering over the text icon. She could send it to her friend right now... or she could see what else she could find first. The thought sparked in her chest, a mix of curiosity and something that felt dangerously like pride.

Ellie smiled faintly and kept scrolling.

Lakeside at Rocky Pointe Golf Club

To Will, the approach to Lakeside at Rocky Pointe Golf Club felt less like pulling into a business and more like entering another world. A grand iron-and-stone gateway spanned the entrance, bronze-gilded letters spelling out *Lakeside at Rocky Pointe.* Lantern posts flanking the drive glowed amber, their light stretching shadows across ivy-clad walls.

Past the gates, the road descended through a corridor of towering oaks, their branches meeting overhead like a cathedral ceiling. Through breaks in the trees, the lake caught the last light of sunset, flashing silver and copper. To the left, fairways rolled out like velvet, the grass immaculate, the sand traps sculpted as if by hand.

The sense of exclusivity sharpened with every turn. Polished signs marked *Members Only, Tournament Pavilion, Marina Access.* Footbridges arched over stone-lined streams, flowerbeds of azaleas arranged with deliberate precision.

The clubhouse rose above the 9th and 18th greens, featuring white stone and dark beams designed to mimic an old-world manor. A circular drive encircled a tiered, lit fountain, luxury sedans and SUVs lined neatly out front. Two valets in pressed uniforms lingered by the entrance, their eyes narrowing at Will's government-issued SUV.

The main lot stretched behind pines, quieter, but just as pristine, with flawless brick pavers. Up close, the clubhouse loomed even larger, broad stone steps leading to glass double doors framed by wrought-iron lanterns. Etched above, the club's crest, a flagstick, crossed irons, and the shimmer of a lake, caught the fading sun.

Beneath the polish, Will felt the weight: wealth, power, secrets. This was more than a golf course. It was a fortress of privilege. And tonight, he wasn't here to play. He was here to pry it open.

The General Manager's office overlooked the range, the fading dusk pooling across the glass like smoke. Inside, Elliot Carrington leaned back in his chair, fatigue etched in the lines of his face. He loosened his tie, exhaling slowly as if trying to push the entire night's chaos out of his chest.

Will didn't sit. He stood in front of the desk, weight forward, tone clipped. "Let's go back to the night of the murders. Anything off? Anyone stand out?"

Carrington gave a humorless chuckle. "They all stood out, Detective. You had half the club out on the balcony, craning their necks to watch. Like it was the damn Masters on TV." He shook his head. "One in particular wouldn't quit, Graham Holloway. He was like a dog with a bone, pressing me for answers I didn't have. What was found, who had access, and if you'd taken or tampered with evidence."

Will's eyes sharpened. "And?"

Carrington hesitated, then leaned forward, lowering his voice. "After the crowd thinned, I checked the locker room. The door was ajar. On the bench was a folded towel with a red smear, looked like a V drawn with lipstick or blood, I couldn't tell. It hadn't been there earlier. My gut says Holloway slipped in. Couldn't resist."

Will's jaw flexed, but he shifted gears. "Who knows the property best? The trails, the sheds, the old tunnels. Every corner someone could slip through?"

That gave Carrington pause. He leaned back again, fingers drumming the desk. "That'd be Eldon Price. My assistant groundskeeper."

"Price," Will repeated.

Carrington nodded. "Strange fellow, but... good at what he does. Hell, better than good. He treats this place like it's sacred ground. Talks about the turf like it's alive. I've seen him crouch over a patch of grass like he's diagnosing a patient. The rest of the staff laugh about it, call him a little too intense, maybe even odd. But I'll say this: nobody knows more about this course than he does. Every blade of grass, every irrigation line, every shortcut."

Will tilted his head. "Eccentric doesn't rule him out."

"I'm not saying he's dangerous," Carrington replied quickly, hands raised. "Just... unusual. Awkward. The kind of man who'll keep to himself unless you ask him about bentgrass seed blends, and then you'll get a half-hour sermon. But if you're looking for someone who notices things around here? Someone who sees what others miss? Price is your man."

Will absorbed that, silent for a moment before nodding. "Then I'll be having a word with him."

Carrington shifted again, unease flickering across his face. "Just don't spook him. The man's loyalty isn't to the members or the club. It's to the land. And when someone's wired like that... you never quite know where their line is."

Will didn't bother with small talk. "Ok, let's switch gears. We've been through the financials: Whitmore, Gilmore, Yates, the whole committee. Money explains most of their votes. But not all of them." He leaned forward, voice low. "What about leverage? Anything that could've pushed a man like Whitmore to break ranks?"

Carrington's smile faltered, just a flicker. "Detective, these are prominent men. Their reputations—"

"That wasn't the question," Will cut in. "I asked if you ever heard of... extracurriculars. Anything they wouldn't want the public to know. Affairs. Deviations. Things that could swing a vote if someone held it over them."

Carrington shifted behind his desk, lowering his gaze. "Clubs like this, discretion is currency. People think the real power is in the balance sheets, but often it's in who knows what about whom. I've... overheard rumors. Encounters with staff. Certain off-book gatherings after charity events. Nothing I could ever prove." He hesitated, then added, quieter, "There were whispers Whitmore shut down a vote once after someone dropped a photo on his desk. No one ever said what was in it. He looked white as chalk."

Will watched him closely. "What about the underground web Steve was running? You know the kind of site I mean. Anything like that tied back here?"

Carrington straightened, defensive now. "If something like that touched the club, it never came across my desk officially. But... Steve had friends here. Staff, even a few low-level members. He liked to make introductions. If you're asking whether men of standing could've found their way onto that site? With the money and appetite involved? It's possible."

Will let the silence stretch long enough that Carrington shifted again, smoothing a crease in his jacket. Finally, Carrington muttered, "This place is built on appearances, Detective. And appearances are only as solid as the secrets they bury."

Outside at the cart shed.

Will found the assistant groundskeeper, Eldon Price, right where Carrington said he would be. Price stood with his hands buried in the pockets of a faded windbreaker, rocking slightly on his heels. His eyes kept flicking toward the door, the path, anywhere but Will, "Mr. Carrington radioed me and said you needed some help from me?" Price coyly asked.

"You worked the north greens the night Whitmore died," Will said, watching him. "Anyone else on that side?"

Price shrugged. "A couple of part-timers. Didn't see much from the talk around here. I saw they messed up that green; we just treated it, rolled it."

From the corner of his eye, Will caught a movement, a maintenance cart rolling by, with a small camera rig bolted to its front frame.

Price followed his gaze. "For the tournaments," he said. "We film every hole, every angle. Members like their highlight reels."

"Where's that footage stored?"

"Wine cellar," Price said, voice low. "Years' worth down there. Not just tournaments, socials, fundraisers, or anything on the grounds. Members only. Just inside the maintenance tunnel."

Before Will could press, his phone buzzed. Kristen.

He stepped aside and answered.

"She's at the pier," Kristen said, her voice clipped. "Ellie. Says she's interviewing a caddy for Emily's research project. Down where some of the golfers come by boat to the course at the marina."

Will closed his eyes briefly. "Tell her to go home. Now. Who is she with?"

Back on the cart path, Price was looking anywhere but at Will. "We done?" he asked.

"Not even close," Will said, but he was already moving toward the clubhouse and saw Casey pulling in from the main entrance roadway.

Golf course – Marina access

Ellie leaned on the pier railing, phone in hand, breeze tugging at her hair. She'd just wrapped what she called "the caddy interview", really just a chat about old club gossip, and now she was thumbing a post into her private feed:

Rich creeps at the country club think they own the world. Bet they'd fold if someone flipped their tables.

She hit "share," smirking.

Ellie looked up to see her mom's SUV pulling up to the marina parking lot. She knew she had been busted.

By sundown, her caption will have been screenshotted twice and passed through three group chats. Somewhere, far from the pier, it landed in the wrong hands once again.

Pickup - Outside the Clubhouse

Will met Kristen in the lot fifteen minutes later, Ellie trailing a few steps behind with her arms folded tight across her chest.

"She was still at the pier when I got there," Kristen said. "Claims she was doing 'research' for Emily."

"I wasn't bothering anyone," Ellie muttered.

"You were bothering me, can't be worrying about you and do my job, what were you told just last night?" Will said flatly. "You stay where we can see you. We've got business in the wine cellar."

Casey was already striding toward the side entrance. Upset with Ellie as well for her blatant disregard of possible danger and seeing that she was tagging along, "Fine. Ellie, you can wait by the tasting room. Just don't touch anything."

Ellie followed them inside at first with her eyes, curiosity written all over her face. When Will and Casey worked on a rusted doorknob at the far wall, she drifted closer, pretending to study the wine racks.

The Wine Cellar

The wine cellar smelled of oak barrels and damp stone, the kind of cool, stale air that hadn't moved in decades. Casey's flashlight beam slid along dusty vintages before catching on a warped door. The lock gave with a metallic sigh. To the right was an air-conditioned room that appeared to contain the recordings Price had mentioned to Will.

"Strange place to store video footage, guess it keeps the server cool?" Casey said out loud.

Beyond it, a broad tunnel extended into the darkness, its walls lined with rough, blackened brick, housing power cables and low LED lighting.

"Prohibition built," Will murmured.

Smugglers used to run liquor through here before the club had its liquor license. The dust on the floor had been disturbed recently, and more than one trip into the tunnel had been made. Now, the crew used it as an underground maintenance tunnel. Will thought this was what it must look like underneath Disney.

Halfway down, the passage opened into a narrow room. The smell hit first, mildew, paper, something sharper beneath it.

Casey's beam landed on the wall. It was a room that was once used for dry goods storage.

Photographs. Dozens of them, taped in precise rows. Victims they recognized, stiff and posed in death. Event snapshots. News clippings. And in the lower corner, two images that made Will's breath lock in his chest.

Ellie.

One shot of her leaning on the pier railing, phone in hand, hair pulled back. Another of her crossing the school parking lot, backpack slung over one shoulder.

"Tell me she didn't post these," Casey muttered.

"I didn't," Ellie said quickly, voice sharp with fear. "I never put those up, and I never saw anyone taking my picture. I swear."

Will's glare lingered on her, his jaw tight, but she stepped closer anyway, scanning the wall. Her fingers stopped on a different photo—not a face, but a splash of painted color on cracked concrete.

"I've seen that," she whispered.

Will's head snapped toward her. "Where?"

"Down by the old maintenance shed," Ellie answered slowly. "A couple of weeks ago, Maya and I were exploring. There's a mural there, half-covered in ivy. This looks just like it."

Will crouched in front of the taped photo, eyes narrowing at the flaking paint.

Casey pulled out her phone, dropped a GPS pin, and typed a note: MURAL — POSSIBLE ACCESS. "If this is the other end of the tunnel," she said, "it's been wide open the whole time. Anyone who knows about it could come and go."

Will rose, the muscle in his jaw working. "And now we know someone's been using it. Not just looking—watching."

Emily's Room

Upstairs, Emily sat cross-legged on her bed, her phone casting a pale glow across her face. At her father's insistence, she was combing through Ellie's feed. Post after post unfurled in her hands—sunset selfies, tagged locations, filtered candids. A breadcrumb trail, each one laid out like coordinates on a map.

Then her thumb froze.

A shot from two weeks ago. Ellie grinning beside Maya, both of them leaning against the same ivy-choked wall. Behind them, barely in frame, the mural, faded color on crumbling concrete. The exact image taped in the tunnel.

Emily's chest constricted. If she could trace Ellie's last month in minutes, then so could he. So could anyone.

She shoved the phone aside and pulled her criminology notes into her lap, flipping to the printout of the tunnel wall photos her dad had just sent to her. Her gaze darted between them and the feed: the pier shot, the school parking lot, the mural half-hidden in ivy. The matches were undeniable.

Her heart pounded so hard it made her fingertips tingle. "He's not just finding her," Emily whispered. "She's giving him a map."

For a moment, she couldn't move. The corkboard upstairs suddenly felt childish, clippings, red string, puzzle pieces that had been safe because they were abstract. This wasn't abstract anymore. This was Ellie, and it was real.

Her breath came short, ragged. She pressed her palms to her eyes as if she could block out the images, but they lingered: Ellie smiling on a pier, Ellie's shoes caught in a grainy video frame, Ellie unknowingly walking straight into his camera lens.

The papers slipped from her hands onto the floor, and she curled her knees up to her chest on the bed. For the first time since she started pinning evidence to her wall, Emily wasn't thinking like a detective. She was thinking like a sister.

And she was terrified. So she picked up her phone and scrolled through the contacts until she found: Detective Murphy.

Sermon #2

Will's phone buzzed with a text alert, the secure alert tagged *High Priority — Cybercrimes Unit.* An encrypted file had been scraped from a fringe video forum, uploaded under an account that hadn't existed twelve hours ago.

Casey leaned against the desk as Will opened it. "If this starts with 'Help me, Obi-Wan Kenobi,' I'm out," she said.

The first three seconds were a black screen and static. Then came The Vicar's voice, distorted and metallic, but spliced with official sound bites.

"Authorities urge members of the finance committee to take precautions..."

Another pause, then Will's voice from a two-day-old interview: "...we'll see who's keeping score."

Over it, the Vicar murmured, low and oily: "*Yes, Detective. And I never miss a stroke... your faith in your friends is your weakness.*"

Casey gave a half-snort. "Great. Did he just go full Palpatine?"

The screen flashed half-second images: floodlit greens, rows of scorecards, a gloved hand painting black letters onto white leather. A faint organ chord repeated four notes over and over, like a funeral march.

Will shut the laptop. "We need to know how he got that press release audio."

Two miles away, Ellie and Emily sat cross-legged on Emily's bed. Ellie was grinning as she turned her phone so her sister could see the video.

"Some guy's making murder TikToks now. This one's got, like, art-house vibes."

Emily watched in silence until the scorecard flashed onscreen, two names she knew had never been released. Andrew Malloy and Kasey Harrow.

Her stomach went cold. "Where did you get this?"

"It's all over my feed," Ellie said, scrolling through comments tagged with skull emojis. "I mean, creepy, but clever."

Emily's voice sharpened. "Ellie, these are case-only details. No one outside the department should know this."

Ellie blinked, thrown by her sister's reaction. "Relax. It's just a video."

Three hours later, Will's phone buzzed again. The second video was shorter —30 seconds —but just as deliberate.

The Vicar's voice: *"Your next hole will be the hardest yet."*

A still shot of a putting green at night filled the screen. In the reflection of the clubhouse window, a figure stood, half-shadowed, wearing a cheer uniform.

Casey squinted. "That's either a cheerleader... or Princess Leia at a pep rally."

Will's jaw tightened. "Trace the source. Now."

The Scorecard Threat

Kristen noticed it the moment she entered the kitchen, placed carefully in the center of the counter. A folded golf scorecard, no envelope, no note.

The overhead light cast a faint sheen across the paper's surface.

She picked it up. It was heavier than a typical card, with stiff, crisp paper and sharp edges that caught her thumb.

When she unfolded it, the scent of ink and a faint metallic smell rose from the page. Her name was written across the top in thick, blocky red letters that almost seemed to glisten.

Kristen's heartbeat quickened. She turned it over.

On the back, only two letters are visible, spaced evenly: **E/E**. She murmured to herself, "Emily... Ellie?" The simpler guess was Emily twice, perhaps a code, maybe a taunt. The Vicar enjoyed playing his games.

Then her gaze shifted to the side, catching the dining chair. Ellie's cheer jacket hung there, sleeves draped as if tossed carelessly.

The white embroidery on the back stood out even from across the room: **E/E**, curling in the same script she'd had stitched before the season started.

Kristen's stomach clenched, a cold feeling spreading quickly.

She carefully set the scorecard down, as if it might bite, already mentally running through chain-of-custody procedures, entry points, and who could have left it there without leaving signs of a break-in. A floorboard creaked overhead.

Kristen's head jerked up, every muscle in her shoulders tightening.

"Ellie?" she called—a pause, then the faint slam of a bedroom door. Relief and irritation tangled in her chest.

"We're going to talk," she muttered, glancing again at the scorecard, at those two letters, then heading for the stairs as she sends Will a text to come home ASAP. Kristen grabbed a knife from the block and went through the house, checking windows and door locks, half of which were unlocked.

Upstairs, Ellie sat cross-legged on her bed, her phone in hand, still wearing her cheer jacket. She'd seen the "cheerleader" footage in her feed earlier, a blurry, low-light clip that ended on her own uniform's white embroidery. She hadn't told her mom.

Instead, she pulled up her private friends-only account and typed:

Come at me.

The post went live with a satisfying little *ding*.

Minutes later, her phone buzzed. A direct message from an account she didn't recognize, no text, just a photo.

Her breath caught.

It was her. Same jacket, same angle... except she hadn't taken it.

Emily's voice came from behind her. "Ellie... how did you take...that's not from your phone."

Kristen walks in and asks, "What's not from your phone?" Ellie turned and showed her mother the photo someone had taken of her at school.

Will's phone chimed; cybercrimes had been notified and intercepted the same image. The tech's voice was tight in his ear: monitoring Kristen, Ellie, and Emily's numbers on Will's request, they were in contact with the phone carrier to give them a heads up on any suspicious numbers or lack thereof, calling any of the phones.

"Sir, we pulled the metadata. Timestamps are from an hour ago; GPS coordinates place it within the course perimeter. South edge, between the twelfth hole and the old maintenance shed."

Will's jaw set. "She's not bait anymore. She's a target."

As he grabbed his coat, he opened the surveillance app tied to their upgraded home security system. It buffered longer than usual. A spinning wheel. Then the feed finally blinked to life, but the upstairs hallway cam, usually fixed at center, was angled too far left, showing only the top of a lamp.

He frowned. The app registered a poor network signal despite a strong reception. A blinking warning: "Sync Error: Reauthentication Required."

Will froze.

"Kristen set this manually last week," he murmured to himself.

Something wasn't right.

He called Casey, voice hard. "We've got a new lead."

Shadow on the Fairway

The image was grainy, pulled from one of the course's perimeter cams, more shadow than substance, but the movement was clear enough.

A slim figure, clad in dark colors, paced along the outer fence line near the eleventh fairway. The way the body shifted weight, the quick turn of the head... it was uncanny.

Casey froze the frame just as the figure vanished into the blind spot near the maintenance shed. "Looks like your kid's twin."

Will leaned closer. "That's not Ellie."

"Then somebody's either studying her TikToks," Casey said, "or we've got a cosplayer with bad intentions."

Will didn't like either option. "Could be he's mimicking her, baiting us."

"Or baiting her."

They exchanged a look, neither one liking where the logic went.

Ten minutes later, they were on the course, weaving through a path cut between low hedges and the fence. Casey swept her flashlight in lazy arcs, the beam catching on clumps of wet grass and a lone beer can.

"This is getting old," she muttered. "We're running around in the dark chasing footprints like a pair of moisture farmers."

Will glanced at her. "You've been on a Star Wars streak lately. What's with that?"

She grinned. "Empowering women, Anderson. Princess Leia took down a slug crime boss in a bikini and chained him with his own leash. You think I can't rock that look?"

Will shook his head. "Not answering that."

She stopped, digging out her phone. "Too late. Visual aid incoming."

Before he could shut her down, Casey thumbed through her gallery and spun the screen toward him. There she was, grinning in the infamous Leia slave bikini, flanked by two equally underdressed Leias, one being Kristen, all three looking like Charlotte-Mecklenburg PD security was seconds away from citing them for indecent exposure. Overhead, a banner screamed *Queen City Con, Charlotte*. Will stared for a beat too long before looking away. "We're working a case."

"And I'm proving a point." She slid the phone back into her pocket with a smirk. "Besides, you're blushing. Man, I love to make the Iron Will blush."

Before he could retort, her radio crackled: "No movement on the west fence. Maintenance crew clear."

Will keyed his mic. "Copy that." He scanned the empty stretch of fairway. "If that wasn't Ellie out here... Kristen's going to think it was."

Casey's smirk faded. "Which means she's about to lock her down like the Death Star trench."

They turned back toward the SUV, the quiet of the course settling in heavy around them. Somewhere behind them, the maintenance shed loomed in the dark, and whoever had slipped past the cameras hadn't left a trace.

Casey Calls Kristen

Kristen was halfway through her second glass of Moscato when her phone buzzed. The caller ID read: Casey M.

"Please tell me this is about dinner," Kristen said, answering.

"Nope," Casey replied, her voice edged with that mix of trouble and amusement Kristen knew too well. "Sending you something. Don't freak out until you've seen it."

The file arrived: security footage from the course perimeter cams. The timestamp was from less than two hours ago.

Kristen squinted at the grainy night image. A figure, female, jogging along the fence line. Slate-grey Lululemon tank. Deep teal Hotty Hot shorts. Black running belt. Nike Pegasus. High ponytail swaying.

Kristen's stomach clenched. "That's Ellie's trail gear.

"Exactly," Casey said. "She went off the grid near the maintenance shed.

Will thinks it could be the killer copying her. Me? I'm not sold."

Kristen's voice dropped. "You think she's reckless."

Casey shook her head. "Not reckless, scared.

Every time she looks at Emily, she remembers what almost happened. So she runs headfirst into danger, because waiting for it to come to her is worse."

Kristen let out a sharp breath. "Where'd this come from?"

"Casey's Fan Club," Casey said dryly. "I've still got admiring friends in IT and surveillance. Figured you'd want to know before Will comes storming home breathing fire."

Kristen sipped her wine, leaning back in her chair. "You know, between this and the time we streaked through my living room in front of him with tequila shots, he's probably reconsidering every life choice he's ever made."

Casey laughed. "That was *your* idea. And it was wine, High Octane Moscato, by the case. Classy streaking."

"Brazilian Girl Power," Kristen said, raising her glass to the phone.

Casey clinked an imaginary glass back. "Exactly. Ugh, now go handle your kid before I have to show up in the Leia bikini again to make a point."

Kristen groaned, remembering Charlotte Comic Con, three Leias deep. "Do *not* tempt me to bring that up to Will. He'll never recover."

"I'm counting on it," Casey said and hung up.

Anderson House — Later That Night

Will had barely taken off his boots when Kristen appeared in the kitchen doorway, a wineglass in hand and a look that said this conversation was *happening now.*

"We need to talk about your daughter."

He straightened. "Which one?"

Kristen stepped in, her hair loose around her shoulders, the glass already half-empty. "The one who wears slate-grey Lululemon tanks, deep teal Hotty Hot shorts, a black running belt, and black-on-white Nikes... and apparently jogs along the golf course at night when she's supposed to be at a friend's house."

Will froze. "How do you know about that?"

Kristen gave a tight smile. "Because Casey sent me the footage."

Will groaned. "Of course she did."

Kristen's smile widened a fraction. "What can I say? We've got a whole sisterhood thing going. And before you ask, yes, we still remember *that night.*"

Will winced, already seeing the memory: Kristen and Casey, both very drunk, both very naked, marching past him without shame, wine bottles in hand, announcing it was *girl power hour* before heading to the pool. He'd learned a long time ago not to argue with that kind of alliance.

"Kristen..." he started, but she cut him off.

"I saw the footage, Will. The figure was wearing *Ellie's exact outfit.* Same ponytail, same stride. You can't tell me that's a coincidence."

Upstairs, a door opened. Ellie appeared at the top of the stairs, earbuds looped around her neck. "You guys talking about me again?"

Kristen's tone sharpened. "Were you near the course tonight?"

Ellie's eyes widened. "What? No. I was at Mia's house. We were watching *Bake Off*. Why?"

"Because someone matching you *exactly* was caught on perimeter cam walking the eleventh fairway," Kristen said.

Ellie shrugged. "So... maybe I have a doppleganger I don't know about?"

Will's gaze didn't leave her. "Maybe it's not a twin. Maybe someone who wants you to be the one they see out there."

Ellie let out a short laugh, but it lacked her usual edge. "Weird flex for a stalker, but whatever. Can I go now?"

She padded back upstairs without waiting for an answer.

Kristen turned back to Will, her voice lower. "If she's lying, I'll know."

"And if she's not..." Will said quietly, "Then the killer just told us he's watching from closer than we thought."

Watcher's Journal

The board lies open across the night, its rank and file shimmering in shadow, pale squares glistening with dew. The wind drifts low across the fairway, brushing the grass in slow waves, like the sweep of a hand over a chess clock.

Pieces scatter, unaware they move to my rhythm. They believe themselves free, unbound, but each step already lies within a pattern.

The Knight vaults first, impulsive, over the fence, blade ready for a phantom enemy. Knights are brave, yes, but blind. They leap into fog, certain their charge will matter, never seeing the snare until it snaps around their throat.

The Queen prowls near the rail, her light flashing in sharp arcs across the darkness. Queens command by presence alone; they burn bright, they claim control. But power invites arrogance, and arrogance drives them into corners where their moves grow limited, desperate.

The King trudges behind, heavy with duty, slow with caution. Kings believe themselves sacred, untouchable, but the board knows better. A King without silence around him is already in check, his every move shackled by the fear of collapse.

The Pawns. Two stand apart., The forward Pawn, loud and restless, forever pressing ahead into open squares, daring the strike that will come., The quiet Pawn, measured, deliberate, stacking her defenses while no one notices. Patient pawns cross the board unseen, and when they reach the far rank, they transform. Into anything. Even into a Queen. She is the one to watch.

And then—an intruder piece. Not blood, not bound, but orbiting their board nonetheless. A Rook. She slides along her lines with speed and strength, never diagonal, never subtle. She crashes through walls, shatters neat patterns, refusing sacrifice, refusing elegance. Rooks are blunt and brutal, a shield to some, a hammer to others. And in endgames, rooks draw blood.

I note her path, her orbit around the King and Queen. Even pawns drift toward her shadow, leaning into the protection she pretends to give.

Two Pawns. A Rook. A Queen. And the Knight, thrashing at phantoms.

They believe the Rook keeps them safe. But rooks fall.

Rooks always fall when the endgame comes.

I close the journal. The board resets. The fairway returns to silence. The family thinks they have survived the night.

They have not.

The game has not yet begun.

Victim Number IV

The sun streamed into the ballroom, which carried a lingering smell of overcooked salmon and spilled wine. Overhead, chandeliers still burned brightly, their glow reflecting off dozens of half-filled crystal glasses resting on linen-covered tables. In the center of the polished dance floor lay Gerald McBride. His charcoal suit was spotless, lapels unrumpled, tie knotted perfectly. His hands were folded neatly over his chest, almost too neatly.

But Will's eyes were fixed on the crimson streak across the torso. This time, it wasn't paint. It was wine, a dark, nearly black cabernet, still trailing down the hem of McBride's jacket in slow, glistening rivulets. Under the harsh overhead lights, the Roman numeral IV shimmered, slick and fresh.

He crouched down, his gaze sharp and methodical. The cufflinks were undisturbed, the shoes immaculately shined, the soles spotless. In his mind, the crime scenes began to stack up, one over the other, like layers of translucent film. "Different," he murmured.

Casey glanced over. "How?"

"No glove. No postmortem posing in an open space; this was inside, under controlled light. And..." Will pointed to the IV. "The last victim was painted with IV...the others had paint, consistent stroke work. This is a pour. The drips are uneven, like it was dumped, not brushed."

"Copycat?" Casey asked, her eyes narrowing. "Or just a different message?"

Will straightened and looked around the room. "If it's a copycat, they have access to the same victim pool. If it's a message, then McBride wasn't meant to be counted the same way as the others."

From across the room, club member and one of the Assistant District Attorneys, Drew Drake, stepped out from a group of uniforms, his face grim, and headed straight for Will and Casey. "McBride was scheduled to testify next week in the toxic waste corruption case, which has been tied up in litigation for years. Half the board was going to be involved in that deposition. He was also previously rumored to be under investigation and facing disbarment due to his involvement in some shady dealings and professional misconduct. He claims to have retired, but I'm sure you can verify this."

Will's gaze shifted to the IV again. "Maybe that's not a number. Maybe it's shorthand for something else entirely. Maybe his misconduct caught up with him."

Later that day

Casey dropped a rubber-banded stack onto the table. "Lakeview archives. Finance minutes. April fourteenth, the night they shoved the multi-million project through."

She flipped to the page and ran a finger down the margin. "Attendance: Whitmore, Gilmore, Yates,

McBride... and a who's who of Oakhaven's old guard." Tap, tap. "Roll-call, recorded those four and the rest of the board:

James R. Calloway—real estate.
Gerald McBride—retired lawyer,
Rumored to have likely been disbarred.
Kasey Harrow—bank VP.
Phil Jones—CPA, resort money.
Andrew Mallory—shipping. All still local."

Casey glanced at the evidence board. "Now watch this, our red numerals on the calling cards go one-for-one with the recorded voting sequence. The clerk basically handed him the list."

Will let out a breath. "So it's not a countdown and it's not random. He's killing his way through that room. Voting order, listed in roman numerals." He met her eyes. "Damn good catch."

"But he's not doing it in order," Casey added. "Which means we can't guess who's next based on the numbers alone."

Will stared at the list again, his gaze locking on Calloway's name, the same one they'd just seen in The Vicar's latest video, still alive.

"Maybe this is about money," he said at last, his voice low, almost to himself. "But who was set to gain... and who was set to lose?"

The question hung heavy in the air, carrying with it three unspoken threads: sexual scandal, cartel involvement, or revenge. Any of them could fit. Any of them could kill.

Will's case notes were half completed when his phone buzzed. Kristen's voice came sharp and hurried through the line. "Ellie never came home after practice."

He straightened instantly. "Emily?"

"She said Ellie was staying at a friend's. I called, but she's not there. She's not answering texts."

Will's thumb flew over his phone screen, pulling up the family location-sharing app. Casey watched the color drain from his face as the map loaded.

"She's not at a friend's," he said. "She's by the golf course. Fence line, near the 14th hole."

Casey was already grabbing her jacket. "Tell me that hardheaded child is not wearing the cheer jacket from the last video."

Will didn't answer. His mind was already moving to the layout of the course, the blind spots along the fence, and the things he'd just learned in the ballroom that might mean the killer was shifting strategy.

Oakhaven High School - The Scorekeeper's Riddle"

Earlier that day, the bell had just rung for the third block when Ellie spotted the envelope waiting on the lip of her locker. Not stuffed inside, not taped, placed. Perfectly square, like someone had measured the angles.

The paper was heavy, cream-colored, embossed faintly with the Oakhaven Club's crest. No address. No stamp.

Her stomach dipped.

She glanced both ways down the hall, kids rushing past with earbuds, laughter bouncing, the chaos of everyday life. Nobody is looking at her. Nobody is slowing down.

Hands tight, she slid the envelope free and tucked it into her bag before anyone could notice.

In the bathroom stall, she peeled it open with shaking fingers. Inside was a golf scorecard: the same stiff, almost metallic-scented paper as the one her mom had found in the kitchen.

Across the top, in thick red ink:

AM / KH

And below it, a single date scrawled in block letters:

SEPT 14

The air in the stall felt suddenly thinner.

Andrew Mallory. Kasey Harrow. She'd seen the names in Emily's notes, whispered in her sister's late-night arguments with their dad. These weren't random letters. They were people.

Ellie's chest thudded. She traced the date with her finger. Tomorrow.

For a moment, she thought of taking it straight to Will, of blurting it out to Emily, to Casey, to anyone. But the thought twisted, sharp.

If she told, they'd lock her down harder. More rules. More eyes. More prison.

She folded the card back into its envelope, slipped it deep into her bag, and washed her hands twice before heading out.

By the time she hit the quad, her grin was back in place. Nobody looking at her would see the sweat clinging to her palms or the way her heart stuttered when she thought of the date.

Tomorrow.

The Scorekeeper wasn't finished.

Finding Ellie

Presently, the fence at the far edge of the golf course was older here; the metal looked dull and splattered with rust, the links loose enough in spots to bend when the wind pushed against them. Beyond it, the 14th fairway sloped gently, dew already gathering under the silver-gray sky.

Ellie had her phone out, with one earbud in and the other dangling against her cheer jacket. The white E/E embroidery caught the low light every time she moved. She wore the same slate-gray Lululemon Swiftly Tech tank and deep teal Hotty Hot shorts she favored for runs; she had two of each since Emily sometimes had to match her, the breeze nudging the loose fabric so the liner flashed pale in the dark. Her black-on-white Nike Pegasus left faint marks in the damp dirt near the fence, a breadcrumb trail for anyone watching.

She leaned forward, resting her arms on the top rail, holding the phone high to angle for the best shot of the glowing fairway behind her.

"Not creepy at all," she muttered, snapping another photo.

Somewhere beyond the 14th hole, a sprinkler hissed to life, then another. The sound masked a softer noise, the faint *click* of metal on metal, like a latch being eased open. Ellie didn't hear it.

She switched the camera to video, grinning at the lens. "Rich creeps still out here playing after dark? Guess I'm about to find out." She posted it to her private feed with the caption: *Tables look different from this side of the fence.*

The screen flashed: **Shared.**

Behind her, deep in the shadows past the cart path, a figure shifted. Not forward, not back, just enough to keep her in sight, watching.

Will's SUV fishtailed slightly as he turned onto the access road, headlights sweeping across empty parking lots and shuttered tennis courts.

"Fence line, 14th hole," Casey read from the map on the phone, bracing one hand against the dash. "Pings are barely moving; she's either standing still or walking in circles."

Will's hands were locked on the steering wheel, jaw tight. "If she's wearing that damn cheer jacket, I..."

"More than likely, and I thought she was supposed to be on the buddy system," Casey cut in. "And if I can spot her from a grainy video, he can spot her from just being in the area."

The course loomed ahead, a patchwork of dark fairways broken by white beams from scattered security lights. As they crested the rise near the 14th, Will killed the headlights and slowed to a crawl.

"There," Casey said, pointing.

Through the fence, maybe sixty yards in, a slim figure leaned against the top rail. Even at this distance, the white embroidery on the jacket's back caught the moonlight like a signal flare. She was holding her phone high, face lit from below by the screen glow.

Will's stomach dropped. "She's broadcasting her position without even knowing it."

He swung the SUV into the maintenance lane, tires crunching on gravel, and hit the brakes. They were out of the car in seconds, boots hitting the ground hard.

"Ellie!" Will's voice cut across the damp night air.

She startled, spinning toward them, but before she could answer, something shifted in the trees beyond the fairway. A shadow, breaking cover just enough to be noticed, then gone again.

Casey's hand went instinctively to her holster. "We've got movement past the cart path."

Will vaulted the fence, boots sinking into the wet grass. "Stay with her," he told Casey without looking back. "I'm going to see if our gallery wants to meet the players."

Will's boots thudded over the fairway, breath fogging in the cool air. The sprinklers hissed somewhere in the distance, masking the rustle of his approach until he was within twenty feet of the cart path. A shadow shifted again, just at the fringe of the rough.

"Got you," he muttered, pushing harder.

The figure turned, startled, and Will launched. They went down hard in the damp grass, Will's shoulder driving into the man's midsection. A muffled *oof* escaped

126

as headphones popped free, a tinny beat spilling into the night.

"Yo, Man! What the hell?" the man sputtered, hands up.

Will blinked. Not a killer. Not even close. Just a middle-aged greenskeeper in a faded Red Sox cap, windbreaker smeared with grass clippings. A mesh trash bag lay in the grass beside him, half-full of paper cups and napkins.

Casey jogged up, gun still low but ready. She took in the scene, Will kneeling over a wiry guy holding a dented rake.

"Wow," she said dryly. "You've mastered the 'tackle first, ask questions never' approach."

Will stood, brushing grass from his knees. "He was standing in the dark, watching."

The greenskeeper frowned. "Watching? I've been picking up trash for the last hour. Storm last night blew over half the bins out past the fence."

Casey smirked as she holstered her Sig. "Easy there, Skywalker. Not everyone in the shadows is Darth Vader."

Will shot her a look. "You want to quote Star Wars, do it after we're sure the Death Star isn't still aiming at my kid," as Will helped the man to his feet.

The greenskeeper muttered something about "psycho, nut cops" under his breath, but Casey was already turning back toward the fence where Ellie waited, her phone clenched in both hands.

The man grunted, stooping to gather the spilled trash bag. "Yeah, yeah. Next time, maybe try a handshake first."

Will turned back toward the mist, scanning the dark again. The sprinklers hissed on, relentless. Whatever shadow he'd chased was gone.

Will's gut still knotted. They might have tackled the wrong guy, but that didn't mean the right one hadn't been watching.

Will fell in step behind Casey as they made their way back toward the fence. The greenskeeper trudged off in the opposite direction, headphones back on, rake swinging loosely in one hand.

Ellie was still by the fence, shifting from foot to foot, phone clutched like a talisman. Her eyes flicked past Will's shoulder toward the retreating man. "Who was that?"

"Not who we were looking for," Will said, his tone clipped. "Let's go, young lady."

As he stepped past the spot where the greenskeeper had been crouched, something caught his eye, a second set of impressions in the damp grass. Narrower, deeper in places where the weight had shifted. These didn't match the tread pattern of the greenskeeper's worn sneakers. They cut diagonally away from the cart path, toward the tree line.

Will crouched, running his hand just above the blades, not touching them, as if he could read the scene without disturbing it. Whoever left these had been standing there for a while... long enough to watch Ellie on the fence. Long enough to move when Will came barreling in. Then that same smell, the perfume from the McBride scene. Woman? Cleaner? Detergent? Familiar but can't place it.

Casey stepped up beside him, following his gaze. "Your force sense is telling you that those aren't from R2-D2 back there."

Will's jaw tightened. "No. Our guy was here."

She glanced back at Ellie, then toward the dark stretch beyond the fairway. "So he saw you coming and bailed. Probably laughing all the way to his evil lair."

Will straightened. "He or she's not done yet."

They got Ellie into the SUV, the fence and the grass falling away behind them, but Will's mind stayed fixed on those faint prints disappearing into the trees.

The Ride Home

They rode in silence for a few minutes, the SUV humming over the road. Ellie sat in the back, her arms folded, her chin lifted as if she were daring either of them to start first.

Will didn't make her wait. "You want to tell me what the hell you were thinking?" His voice was low and controlled, yet it carried the weight that made her shoulders pull in. "After everything that's happened, after everything you've seen, you decide to sneak out and go alone, on this golf course? At almost nightfall?"

"I wasn't..." she started, but Casey twisted in her seat, cutting her off.

"No," Casey said flatly. "You were. And you know it." Her eyes narrowed. "Do you remember what happened to your sister in that house? She got gut-punched, dazed, and stripped of her underwear outside your mother's bedroom door. Steve would've finished it if your mom hadn't, by God's saving grace, accidentally been there."

Ellie's gaze flicked away, jaw working.

"And your mom?" Casey's voice softened, but only just. "Drugged. Assaulted. By the same man. You think we want to see that happen again? You think I want to see it happen to you? There are monsters among us, and everyone is sus! You can't go around being so naïve, reckless, and alone."

Will's hands tightened on the wheel. "I will not bury anyone in this family, Ellie. Not you. Not Emily. Not your mother. And if you think I'm overreacting, you don't understand the kind of people we're dealing with."

Ellie's bravado faltered, her voice dropping. "I just... I thought maybe I could help."

"You help by staying alive," Will said, eyes locked on the road. "Not by painting a target on your back."

In the rearview, her eyes looked shinier than she wanted him to see. She muttered something that might've been "Okay, I'm sorry," but it was quiet, and it didn't erase the worry sitting like a stone in Will's gut.

The SUV turned toward home, but the faint imprints in the grass and the way they vanished into the tree line stayed burned into his mind. Whoever had been there was close, close enough to watch. Close enough to wait.

When they pulled into the driveway, the porch light cast a gentle glow over the steps, and the kitchen light spilled across the lawn like a warm welcome.

Kristen was at the counter when they walked in, her reading glasses resting low on her nose, case files spread out beside a mug that had gone cold. She immediately looked up, scanning their faces, her eyes lingering on Ellie.

"Everything okay?" she asked, casual in tone but with that undercurrent that made Ellie pause in the doorway.

Will set his keys down, the metallic clink sharper than it needed to be. "We need to talk about where your daughter's been tonight."

Kristen's gaze moved between them, settling on Ellie. "Where were you?"

Ellie hesitated. "I went to Christi's after practice and I just... went for a run."

"At night? Near the course?" Kristen's voice edged sharper. Her glance toward Will made it clear she already suspected the answer.

Casey lingered near the fridge, voice low. "She was out there when he was. We've got footprints to prove it."

Ellie's arms crossed in that defensive way she had, but Will didn't give her room to retreat.

Before Kristen could speak, Casey stepped closer to her, leaning in to murmur just above a whisper, "I reminded her about Emily, what Steve did to her... and to you. She needed to hear it."

Kristen's expression softened just slightly. She turned back to Ellie, her voice steady but not unkind. "What Casey told you was because she cares about you. She's not apologizing for that, and she shouldn't have to. She loves you, Ellie. That's why she scared you with reality."

Ellie shifted, her eyes darting to Casey, then down to the floor. Her voice was quiet. "I get it."

Will's jaw stayed tight, but the heat in the room shifted, less about anger now, more about keeping the circle unbroken.

Kristen reached out, resting her hand briefly on Ellie's arm. "Then prove you get it. No more runs near the course. No more breaking the rules we have set. Not until this is over."

Ellie nodded once, and for the moment, that was enough. She headed upstairs to her room, sniffled, and quiet sobs formed and squeaked from her.

Will scrubbed a hand down his face and muttered, "I'm getting too old for this shit."

Casey smirked without missing a beat. "Okay, Sergeant Murtaugh. Want me to get you a cardigan and a rocking chair, too?"

The line cracked the tense air like glass underfoot. Kristen barked out a laugh, Casey doubled over, stomping her foot, and even Will, shaking his head, felt the corner of his mouth twitch despite himself.

Upstairs, with tears in her eyes, Ellie dropped her bag onto the bed, tossed in a fresh change of clothes and a sleep shirt, the envelope wedged deep between the math binder and her cheer shoes. Her fingers lingered on the zipper, tugging it just enough closed.

The door cracked open without a knock. Emily leaned in, hair tied back, notebook under her arm.

"You've been acting weird since school," she said. "What's in your bag?"

Ellie's throat tightened. She shrugged, forcing a smirk. "Geometry homework. You want to check my proofs?"

Emily stepped closer, scanning the bag like she could see through it. She reached for the zipper.

Ellie's hand shot out, too fast. "Seriously? Ever heard of privacy?"

Emily froze, eyebrows rising. "So defensive. What are you hiding?"

"Nothing," Ellie said. She laughed, but the sound was brittle. She grabbed the bag and swung it over her shoulder. "I'm late. Mom's pissed at me, so Mia's picking me up. Apparently, I need to be watched, and her mother is into everyone's business, so no privacy there either!"

Emily studied her, noting the way Ellie's grip tightened and the rush in her voice. Something was wrong; she could feel it, but Ellie was already brushing past, perfume and static in her wake.

Left alone, Emily stood in the room a moment longer, staring at the door. She thought about her notes, about the names she'd written down, the pattern she swore she was close to solving.

Number III - The Third Stroke

The beams from the floodlights cut long shadows across the fifth fairway, bleaching the sand of the bunker into something ghostly. Will Anderson ducked under the yellow tape, his boots crunching over damp turf as CSU worked in quiet, gloved precision.

Andrew Mallory, youngest ever to sit on the club board, thirty-three and smug about it, knelt half-propped in the sand trap like some grotesque monument. His body had been forced onto all fours, spine bowed, pants shoved down around his knees. A broken rake shaft jutted up through Mallory's chest and out his collarbone, pinning him in place like a specimen mounted for display.

Casey crouched low, grimacing as her flashlight swept the details. "Holy cow. That's a statement."

She tilted her head, lips tightening. "Looks like somebody went full Darth Maul, cut down and left for display."

Will gave her a flat look. "You realize Maul was cut in half, right?"

Casey stood, brushing grit from her knee. "Details, Anderson. It's still Star Wars ugly."

He exhaled through his nose, his gaze returning to the body. "Ugly, yeah. But not fiction."

On his head, tilted forward so his chin nearly touched the sand, rested a golf cap. Painted across the bill in dripping black strokes: III.

Will shifted closer. For a moment, beneath the reek of blood and paint, something brushed his senses, faint, fleeting, like perfume caught on the air. It was gone almost instantly, carried off by the breeze, but it left the hair at the back of his neck standing on end. As if whoever had been here minutes ago still lingered in the shadows.

Casey's voice broke his focus. "Detective, you're gonna want to see this."

She held up a clear evidence bag. Inside was the folded scorecard, Mallory's name written neatly across the front. On the back, in block red ink, five words bled into the cardstock:

SHE BLACKED OUT, YOU BLED OUT.

Casey exhaled hard, her disgust evident. "That accusation from a few years ago... his daughter's roommate. Either roofied or drunk, depending on who you ask. And the DA's office dropped it for 'insufficient evidence.'"

Will's jaw clenched. "Looks like someone didn't forget."

A crime tech straightened from behind the body, holding something gingerly between tweezers. A golf tee, blood-red, lacquer chipped, wedged cruelly between Mallory's exposed buttocks.

"Son of a bitch," Casey muttered. "He's mocking him. Mocking us."

Will stood, his eyes scanning the tree line beyond the fairway, shadows shifting where the floodlights couldn't reach. "Not mocking," he said quietly. "Preaching."

The coroner's van idled up the cart path. CSU kept working. The fairway bunker that had once been another board member's playground was now another number, another sermon.

Will lingered at the edge of the sand, that faint trace of perfume still in his head. Just a whisper on the breeze, too fleeting to place, but enough to remind him they weren't alone out here.

Casey came up beside him, arms crossed. "Another Roman numeral. Another scorecard. Another ghost."

Will's eyes stayed on Mallory's body, pinned in the sand like a broken animal. "And a message that isn't just about him. Whoever's running this game... they're not done."

Ghost Scent

The bullpen smelled of burnt coffee and printer toner, the low hum of keyboards filling the late hour. Will dropped into his chair, elbows braced on the desk, Mallory's scorecard still sealed in plastic in front of him. The red words seemed to bleed through the bag:

SHE BLACKED OUT, YOU BLED OUT.

Casey set a file down with a snap. "Mallory had cartel whispers all over him. Shipping contracts, off-book containers, phantom bills of lading. And then the sexual assault rumor from his daughter's roommate? Fits the M.O. Cain loved. Fits Steve, too."

Will rubbed a hand across his jaw. "Mallory's not just a number. He was chosen."

Casey sighed. "So was Whitmore. So was Gilmore. So was Yates. Every damn one of them's tied to the finance committee, the land deal, sexual deviances, or worse. Doesn't make the board any shorter."

Will didn't answer right away. His gaze stayed fixed on the scorecard, though his mind drifted back to the fairway bunker. To that moment when the blood and paint had almost drowned his senses, and then, under it, something else.

"I caught a scent tonight," he said finally, voice low.

Casey frowned. "What kind of scent?"

"Perfume. Faint. Sweet. Not from the scene. Just... hanging there. Like someone had been close, just out of sight."

Casey leaned back in her chair, arms crossed. "You sure it wasn't one of the CSU techs? Coroner? Hell, even a bystander too close to the tape?"

"Could've been, a ghost scent," Will admitted, though his voice was flat. "But it didn't feel like it."

Casey raises an eyebrow. "A ghost scent? What are you now, a Jedi Knight? Going to close your eyes and 'feel the Force'?"

Will deadpans: "Better than ignoring it."

Casey: "Next thing I know, you'll be waving your hand at suspects, telling them, 'These aren't the crimes you're looking for.'"

Will let the silence stretch before replying. "Sometimes it's the thing that doesn't belong that matters most."

Casey looked at him for a beat longer, then pushed the file toward him. "You trust your nose, I'll trust the paper trail. Let's see which one gets us there first."

Will didn't push it. But as he reached for the folder, the phantom sweetness clung in his memory, nagging like the ghost of someone who had stood just outside the light.

The Darkness Still Creeps

The conference room reeked of stale coffee and fried food from the night shift. Case files spread out across the table, CSU photos scattered among them. The hum of the fluorescent lights was the only sound until Will dropped the hospital reports into the middle of the chaos.

"Same pattern," he said, voice flat. "Multiple girls have been admitted to Oakhaven General over the past year. All with gaps in memory, tox screens coming back inconclusive. Each one returned to her dorm or apartment with her clothing adjusted, fuzzy or no memory, and no idea who touched her."

Casey flipped the stack, scanning with her detective eyes, taking in everything. Her jaw tightened. "They're using short-life compounds. Burn off in the system before labs can lock on. It's calculated."

Will's eyes lingered on one report, the name jumping out like a bruise: Jordan Hayes. Former cheerleader. A senior when Emily and Ellie were freshmen. A curly blonde with a radiant smile, a headstrong girl who used to sit on their couch during study nights, loud with laughter and lip gloss, now reduced to a redacted incident number.

He felt his stomach knot. "This one's personal. Jordan Hayes. She was around my girls. I'm not letting this sit."

Captain Monroe leaned back, folding his hands over his gut. "And you're sure it isn't just hazing? College parties, blackout drinking—"

Casey cut him off, sharper than intended. "No. It's cartel. The same cocktail moving through our golf course is moving through their veins. This isn't some frat prank."

She slapped down another photo, CSU's haul from Victoria Yates's purse at the chapel. Condoms in a trail, a pill vial tucked beneath them. The lab report stamped across the page.

"Not prescriptions," Casey said. "Designer knockoffs. South American labs. The same supply chain is tied to the land deal; somehow, we haven't nailed it down yet. It's there. Same people laundering money through Rocky Pointe."

Will rubbed the bridge of his nose, the weight of it settling in. Yates's murder wasn't just revenge or ritual; it was a breadcrumb pointing back to the same poison that killed his city and nearly killed his family once before.

"I'll pay Jordan a visit," he said quietly. "Hear it from her directly."

Casey leaned back, arms crossed, the scorecards spread between them. "So is the Vicar's staging sermons while the cartel's staging victims. Different pulpits, same congregation. Are we missing something?"

Will didn't answer. He just stared at Mallory's card one more time, the words bleeding through the plastic:

SHE BLACKED OUT, YOU BLED OUT.

Jordan Hayes

The dorm common room smelled faintly of popcorn and perfume, posters peeling from the cinderblock walls. Jordan Hayes sat curled on a worn couch, sleeves tugged over her hands. She looked older than Will remembered, not in years, but in weight, freshman fifteen, got him almost each year.

She gave him a nervous smile. "Will, I mean Mr. Anderson. Weird seeing you here, huh? I used to cheer with your girls."

Will nodded, easing into the chair across from her. "You did. You can call me Will. I remember you girls all had a pool party and sleepover at our house, your senior year. They still talk about the time you burned the popcorn and set off the alarm."

That pulled a small laugh, but it faded quickly. Silence stretched before Will leaned forward. "Jordan, I've read the report, that is why I called. I need to hear it from you."

Her eyes dropped to her lap. "It was after a mixer. Not even a crazy night. One drink, maybe two. And then... nothing. Just black." She gripped her sleeve tighter. "When I woke up, I was in my own bed. Clothes on, shoes by the door. Like I'd walked myself home."

Will's jaw tightened. "But you didn't."

Jordan shook her head. Her voice lowered, hesitant, as if each word cost her something. "I went to shower, and I couldn't remember... I thought my underwear was inside out. Same color on both sides, so maybe not. But I couldn't remember. Couldn't think straight." She swallowed hard. "There were marks, little crescent scratches on my stomach and under my left breast, like fingernails. My wrists hurt for two days, as if somebody or something had been wrapped around them, holding me down. And I was sore, lower, raw... down here." She pressed a hand lightly against her abdomen. "It felt wrong."

Her voice thinned, brittle with anger. "But the strangest part? I woke up feeling... relaxed. Like I'd just slept on a cloud. Except my head was foggy. It didn't match. None of it matched."

That's when my roommate Jenny told me about this chatroom thread she'd found, girls talking about blacking out, having these out-of-body moments, losing hours like they'd just... slipped away. She said I should get checked, that maybe someone had drugged me.

So I went. I did all the tests. The hospital told me no. No drugs. No signs of anything. Just me, sitting there with this knot in my stomach and nothing to hold onto but my own fear. I filed a report, but it felt empty, as if I were reporting a ghost. They looked at me like maybe I'd just had too much to drink, like it was all my fault for not being able to handle it.

Will let the words hang, fighting the urge to clench his fists. He thought of Emily and Ellie, study nights, laughter, Jordan kicking off her sneakers at their back door, jumping in their pool, and a splash competition.

"Jordan," he said carefully, "we believe it wasn't random. The same people tied to Rocky Pointe and the land deal are moving product through this town. Designer drugs. Hard to trace."

Her head snapped up, eyes wide. "So it wasn't me?"

"No," Will said firmly. "It wasn't you."

For a moment, she just sat there, tears brightening her eyes but not falling. Then she whispered, "I thought I was going crazy."

Will stood, placing his card on the table. "You weren't. And you're not alone. If you remember anything, a smell, a face, a sound, you call me. Day or night. That's my personal cell number."

She nodded, clutching the card like a lifeline.

As Will left the dorm, the laughter of other students drifted from down the hall. Normal, ordinary, untouched. He tightened his jaw. Whoever was behind this wasn't just leaving bodies in bunkers and chapels. They were walking in his daughters' world, poisoning it from the inside.

No Trace

Casey leaned against the edge of Will's desk, coffee cooling in her hand as he finished recounting Jordan Hayes's story. Her face, usually sharp with sarcasm, was tight and flat.

"She thought her underwear was inside out?" Casey asked quietly.

Will nodded. "Same color both inside and out. She couldn't be sure. Couldn't remember, wasn't paying attention. She had scratches on her stomach and under her breast. Wrists sore for two days. Lower abdominal pain. But she also woke up... calm. Relaxed. Like it was staged to feel normal. Only her head was foggy."

Casey swore under her breath, set the coffee down harder than she meant to. "That's chemical engineering. A cocktail built to wipe memory, relax muscles, and metabolize fast enough to dodge a tox screen. It's not amateur. Wrists strapped, like they had her in one of those harnesses."

Will slid the crime scene photo across the desk, the pill vial found in Victoria Yates's purse. "Sound familiar?"

Casey scanned the report, her finger tapping the page. "Designer knockoffs. South American labs. These are the same compounds DHS flagged last month. The cartel isn't just running cash and cocaine through Rocky Pointe. They're distributing rape kits."

Her voice cracked sharply on the last words, then steadied again. "Jordan's story isn't an outlier. It's a business model."

Will sat back, jaw tight, the weight of it pressing down. Jordan was like an older sister to Emily and Ellie, as she had been mentoring them since middle school. Now she's in a dorm, waking up wrong, thinking she's crazy." He rubbed a hand over his face. "This isn't random."

Casey's eyes narrowed, steel creeping into her voice. "Then we treat it like what it is, organized assault with cartel logistics, dark web videos. And if Yates was holding their supply when she died? Someone wanted her silenced."

For a moment, the bullpen noise dropped away, just the two of them in the hum of fluorescent lights.

Will finally spoke. "Then it's not just about catching the Vicar. We're at war with the network Steve left behind."

The Collector's Board

The corkboard wasn't in a bedroom or a dorm. It hung in a windowless room lit by a single desk lamp, the glow swallowing the edges of the space.

Photos were pinned in neat, deliberate rows: Whitmore's crime scene. Gilmore on the range. Yates is in the chapel. The arrangement wasn't guesswork. It was exact.

At the center of the table lay a glossy printout: Emily Anderson's corkboard, captured not from a direct photo, but from the blurred reflection in a bedroom mirror, a sliver she'd overlooked when she posted the image online. The pins and threads were all there, just as she'd arranged them. But in this version, new pieces had been added, connections she hadn't yet made.

Around the edges of the photo, other details emerged: the soft curve of her desk lamp, the hoodie crumpled over her chair, the open notebook still turned to a half-written page. Things that hadn't appeared in the post. Things no social media app had permission to see.

The Collector especially liked the way she moved around the room, pacing, pausing, and studying her board as if it held something sacred.

He watched her think. Watched her wrestle with secrets she hadn't told anyone, not even her father. The kind of thoughts people don't say out loud.

It wasn't just about what she shared. It was about what she thought she kept to herself.

Technology had limits. Obsession didn't. And with the right kind of money, even locked doors meant nothing. Security systems blinked blind. Spy cameras slipped into the smallest, safest places.

They'd paid him to watch her.

At first, it was about protection, making sure she didn't stumble into something delicate. The girl had a habit of being in the wrong place, at the wrong time, listening when no one thought she was—pinning things to her little board. Names, dates, whispers pulled from behind closed doors. She was sniffing too close to something real, the Vicar on her radar, yes, but worse: their plans. The ones that ran deeper, with sharper teeth.

Her sister didn't help, broadcasting bits of Emily's obsession to the world, one filtered photo at a time. The wrong eyes noticed. Flags were triggered.

But watching Emily became something else.

She exposed more than she realized. The way she paced when she thought no one could see. The way she bit her lip when she solved something. The way she undressed in the mirror's reflection, she was too distracted to close the blinds, and the cameras didn't care. Every angle of her life unfolded like a secret she didn't mean to share, and he took it all in.

She was clever, yes. But careless in the ways that made his job easier, and far more enjoyable.

They'd told him to monitor, paid well, cartel money.

He watched.

And some nights, when she moved just right, or leaned too close to the corkboard in nothing but a T-shirt and bare legs, it hardly felt like surveillance at all.

She made it so easy.

And if she got too close to the truth?

Well. Collateral damage was always part of the job, and he decided how to manage it.

Back on his board, a photo of Andrew Mallory at a club banquet. A copy of his shipping manifests. A clipped headline about a college assault allegation. Each item was placed with surgical precision, as though correcting what Emily had missed, filling in the gaps she wasn't supposed to find at all.

A gloved hand reached out, adjusting the alignment of a notecard until it was perfectly parallel with the edges of the board. Then, with deliberate weight, he took a black marker and drew a thick, heavy circle around Emily Anderson's name in the corner.

The pen tapped twice against the paper. A silent punctuation. A decision.

He stepped back, admiring the mirrored corkboard, hers and his, twin puzzles on opposite sides of the glass. Her questions, his answers. Her curiosity, his control.

She thought she was building something in secret.

She had no idea she was already inside the frame.

Watchers Journal - The Hidden Move

The board tilts when the pawns begin to lie.

The forward Pawn has taken my gift and tucked it into her satchel like contraband. She thinks no one saw. She believes she chose secrecy.

But pawns do not choose. They are moved.

Her sister, the quiet Pawn, sniffed close, hand on the zipper, eyes sharp, sensing the danger. She is a cautious one, a student of position. If allowed to cross unnoticed, she could one day crown herself with power. That cannot be permitted.

The Rook circles still, loud and certain, smashing walls with her stride. She is the only piece that makes my calculations stumble. The others fall into their squares neatly, predictably, pliantly. The Rook refuses symmetry. She would burn the board to prove she could.

The King trudges heavily, blind to the file where the threat advances. The Queen flares and dims, torn between fury and fear. Their weight slows them. They cannot keep up.

But the Pawn, my Pawn, presses forward into the open, clutching her riddle, convinced she alone can rewrite the match. Pawns who run ahead meet the blade first. Pawns are always the first to fall.

And yet... she amuses me.

I close the journal, mark the date, and reset the board. The forward Pawn has moved.

The game waits to answer.

Marked

Forensics Breakthrough

Will was halfway through a bitter cup of precinct coffee when the lab call came through.

The tech didn't bother with pleasantries. "We've got a match on the prints from the shed tools."

Will set his cup down. "Go on."

"Eldon Price. He's not in CODIS, that's the national Combined DNA Index System, but the South Carolina Law Enforcement Division, SLED, had him on file. The prints came from a concealed carry permit application he filed about thirteen years ago. It was denied for lack of cause, but the fingerprints stayed in their database."

Casey leaned against her desk, eyebrows raising. "He works there, but our twitchy groundskeeper just got a lot more interesting."

Will frowned, rubbing his thumb along the side of the coffee cup. "Or not. He handles the shed tools every day. His prints being on them doesn't prove intent, just that he was doing his job. Half the maintenance crew's DNA could be on those handles if we bothered to swab."

The tech cleared his throat. "That's not all. We pulled a partial that doesn't match Price or anyone else in the system. Not CODIS, not state. Unknown."

That straightened Will's posture. "Unknown?"

"Clean ridge pattern, high quality. Whoever left it wasn't wearing gloves, and it's recent. Within the last forty-eight hours."

Casey tilted her head, eyes narrowing. "So Price's prints belong there, but someone else's don't. Someone else handled those tools, and wasn't supposed to."

Will exhaled through his nose, uneasy. "Price is too easy a suspect. Guy's awkward, maybe shady, but right now I don't see him as the hand behind any of this." He paused, recalling the wary look in Price's eyes during their interview, the rake flexing in his grip like it was the only anchor he had. "No priors, no history. Just... off."

Casey smirked, though her eyes stayed sharp. "You've got a soft spot for the quiet weirdos, don't you?"

"I've got a soft spot for evidence," Will shot back. He tapped the desk with his finger. "And until we know whose print that is, we're chasing the wrong man."

DHS Intel Drop

They didn't have to wait long before the other shoe dropped. Rivers from DHS called that afternoon, voice tight, *swing by when you get a chance*, the voicemail said.

"Your guy's not just pulling weeds for a paycheck," Rivers said. "We've been tracking a network laundering cartel's cash through luxury club events in the Southeast. Price's name came up in financial patterns we flagged months ago."

Rivers warns, *"Price wasn't their only channel. Someone else at that club is still moving their money, we don't know who."*

Casey straightened. "Patterns like what?"

"Three offshore accounts in the Caymans, two in Belize. All tied to shell corps that 'donate' six figures at charity auctions. Then the money gets washed as prize payouts or capital improvements. And your club's been on that donor rotation twice in the last five years."

Will rubbed the bridge of his nose. "Fake IDs?"

"Two, confirmed. Both match aliases on trafficking manifests from a Florida case last year. We thought he was a facilitator, now I'm thinking he's a hub."

Casey swore under her breath. "So the guy watering the fairways might also be greasing cartel shipments. Did we ever check out that other guy, Gregory, Gregory Young?"

"No, but he's next up in the batter's box to be questioned," Will said.

Casey's Quiet Share with Kristen

On their way back from DHS, Casey dropped Will at the precinct, claiming she had errands. Instead, she swung by the Anderson house, where Kristen was working in the home office.

Casey leaned against the doorframe. "We need to talk about Ellie."

Kristen looked up, wary. "What now?"

"She's been posting little 'come and get me' taunting nuggets online, and I'm afraid for her, being a kid and not realizing the gravity of her actions. I'm sorry, but I had to remind her what happened to Emily, the gut punch, the strip-down, and what Steve did to you. I didn't sugarcoat it."

Kristen's expression softened, but her voice stayed firm. "Good. She needs to hear it from more than just me. And she doesn't need an apology from you for scaring her. She needs to know you said it because you love her."

Casey nodded. "I do. And I can't bear the thought of working another scene where she's the one on the ground."

Kristen crossed the room and wrapped Casey in a hug, her voice trembling. "I had a nightmare last night that Steve came to take them. I couldn't stop him—just stood there, helpless. But then you appeared, like a battle angel glowing lime green, shouting 'For Alderaan!' and suddenly he was gone. Everything was better."

She pulled back slightly, her voice breaking with gratitude. "Someone was watching over us when they put you in our lives. Thank heavens for you, my friend. I'm so grateful you love my girls—our girls."

Casey leaned back to meet Kristen's eyes. "You're family to me. Every girl needs a badass friend running around in her underwear, fighting monsters to keep her grounded—and maybe run naked with her through the yard once in a while. I'd do anything for those girls. Anything. I'd kill for those girls."

Kristen nodded, gathering herself, and shrugged off the tension she had let build up. "I need a drink, want one too?"

"Just one, can't have will gawking at us if we get too deep into that case you just pulled that bottle from." Casey said jokingly.

Sister vs. Sister

Upstairs, Emily sat cross-legged on her bed, a spiral notebook open in front of her, Post-its fanned across the comforter like a deck of cards. She was halfway through penciling in another date on her hand-drawn timeline when a shadow crossed the doorway.

Ellie leaned against the frame, arms folded tight, her jaw set. "You told Casey about my posts."

Emily looked up, the pencil still between her fingers. "Yeah," she said flatly, closing her laptop with one hand. "Because you're playing with fire."

"I'm not stupid," Ellie shot back, stepping into the room. "I'm baiting him. If he's watching me, we can—"

"—get you killed?" Emily cut in, the words sharp. She tossed the pencil aside and stood, closing the gap between them. "This isn't one of your online debates where you 'own' some troll in the comments. This guy isn't hiding behind a screen name. He's already killed people, Ellie."

Ellie's chin lifted, stubborn, but her gaze flicked away. "You think I don't know that? I'm not afraid of him."

"You should be," Emily said, her voice low now, almost pleading. "Because right now? You're not a profile to him. You're a target."

A floorboard creaked in the hall. Neither of them turned until Will's voice cut in from the doorway.

"What did you just say?"

Emily froze. Ellie glanced over, defensive instinct kicking in. "Dad, No, it's not what you think—"

"It's exactly what I think," Will said, stepping into the room. His expression was stone, but his voice had that sharp edge they both recognized. "You've been out there, posting, trying to draw him in?"

Ellie swallowed. "I was careful—"

"Careful?" Will's voice rose. "Careful is staying off the radar. Being careful does not make you the next name on his list. We've got three bodies in the ground and you're—" He stopped himself, dragging a hand down his face. "You're not bait. You're my daughter. You are a teenage girl."

Ellie opened her mouth, but Emily's quiet, "She thinks she's helping," cut in.

Will's eyes didn't leave Ellie. "Helping is giving us a lead, not giving him a target. This ends now. No more posts. No more games. I find out you've been near that course again, we're going to have a different conversation."

Ellie dropped her gaze. Will turned and left before she could answer, his footsteps heavy on the stairs.

Emily sank back onto her bed, staring after him. Ellie stood there a moment longer, arms still crossed, but the defiance in her eyes was thinner now, and something else had crept in.

Ellie lingered in Emily's doorway long after Will's footsteps faded. Her arms were still crossed, but the hard edge in her face was softer now, the tiniest crack in her defiance.

Downstairs, the murmur of voices drifted up, Casey's, low and measured, and Kristen's quieter replies.

"You lit into her?" Kristen asked, leaning one shoulder against the kitchen doorway, wine glass in hand.

"Like I said, I reminded her what happened to Emily," Casey said. "And to you. She's smart, but she's young. She thinks she's untouchable. I didn't like her attitude when we found her on the course." Casey's mouth twitched into a half-smile. "Guess I'm just better with bullets than teenagers."

Kristen smirked. "You said the same thing the night we streaked past Will in nothing but liquid courage and girl power."

Casey grinned. "Yeah. And I still maintain the pool was a tactical advantage, sober or not."

At the end of the hall, Will appeared, having caught just enough to know he'd regret hearing the rest. The words "liquid courage" and "girl power" triggered an unwelcome mental flashback to that night during the Julien and Steve cases, Casey and Kristen, laughing like maniacs as they strolled past him toward the pool, naked and clutching a bottle. He'd been trying to scrub that memory ever since.

He muttered something that sounded suspiciously like "too old for this" under his breath and kept walking toward his office.

Kristen tipped her glass toward the ceiling, where the faint creak of Emily's floorboards carried through. "They'll figure it out. Just... not tonight."

Watcher's Journal — The Rook's Defiance

The board should be clean. Orderly.

Every square has a purpose. Every piece is confined to its pattern. Every move is written before it is made.

But the Rook disturbs it.

She does not glide in straight lines tonight. She breaks the geometry.

Her path slants where no slant should exist. She collides into files meant to remain untouched, reshaping the pattern with brute force. She laughs when silence is required, taunts when fear should still her tongue.

She shields when no one asks her to. She dares the King to scold, then turns and shields him harder, as if defiance itself is her weapon.

This is not her board. She is not blood, not bound by blood.

And still, she plays as if it is hers to command.

Knights, I can predict, they always leap into traps, noble and blind.

Queens, I can bait, arrogant, proud, burning their power too fast in one direction.

Kings, I can corner, slow, burdened, already in check from the moment they move.

Pawns, I can herd, restless or patient, it does not matter. They all reach the same end.

But the Rook— The Rook does not play the game. She smashes   through   it. She redraws the edges of the board with her defiance, daring me to make sense of her chaos.

Worse:

The Pawns watch her. They lean toward her shadow more than the King's command or the Queen's fury. She bends them to her tempo. She makes them think survival lies in her wake.

I redraw my lines. Adjust my calculations. Still, her next strike remains hidden from me.

That is intolerable.

An unchecked Rook threatens the endgame. A Rook that cannot be predicted must be removed.

And soon.

Shadow on the Rook

The driving range stretched out pale under the fog, rows of empty tees and scattered balls glowing faintly in the sodium light.

Will's boots crunched on the gravel path as he moved between the stalls, flashlight beam sweeping slow arcs across the mats. Everything looked orderly, buckets stacked, dispenser locked, the silence almost clinical.

He crouched near the edge, examining a fresh scuff in the dirt. Could've been a shoe. Could've been nothing. He made a mental note, marking it down the way he always did. Methodical. Step by step. No leaps, no hunches.

The driving range stretched pale under the fog, rows of empty tees and scattered balls glowing faintly in the sodium light.

Will's boots crunched on gravel as he moved between the stalls, flashlight beam sweeping slow arcs across the mats. Everything looked orderly, buckets stacked, dispenser locked, the silence clinical.

He crouched at the edge, eyeing a fresh scuff in the dirt. Could've been a shoe. Could've been nothing. He logged it away, methodical as ever, one square at a time.

Across the course, Casey slipped between the buggies in the cart shed. Shadows pooled deep here, the smell of gasoline and damp grass clinging to the air. Her flashlight bounced off a cracked windshield, flaring like a stormtrooper's helmet. She cut the beam, lips quirking.

"Great," she muttered to herself. "All I need is a Jawa popping out of the dark."

She moved deeper, free hand brushing the butt of her Sig. The old corrugated doors creaked with the breeze, wrong rhythm, like someone breathing through a mask. The hair at her neck prickled.

"Death Star trench run, all over again," she whispered. "And I left my X-wing at home."

She stopped dead center, holstered the flashlight, and drew the Sig instead. Her voice dropped to a grin. "Fine. You want me to play Luke Skywalker? Come on then. Let's see if you hit me, or if you're just another stormtrooper."

The wind shoved harder, rattling the metal panels. Sprinklers hissed to life somewhere downrange, masking the silence that followed.

A few minutes later, Will and Casey converged at the clubhouse side path.

"Range was clean," Will reported. "Fresh scuff, but could've been maintenance."

Casey slid her Sig back into its holster, eyes still on the shadows. "Cart shed's clear, too. Unless you count the feeling I wasn't the only one in there. Whole place had Vader breathing vibes."

Will gave her a look, not disbelief, not exactly, but wary. "Paranoia or instinct?"

"Instinct," Casey said flatly. "And it hasn't been wrong yet. Ask Han Solo, 'never tell me the odds.'"

Will exhaled, checked his watch. "Gregory Young's shift is nearly over. Let's catch him before he disappears."

Casey smirked as they started toward the glow of the clubhouse. "Fine. But if a guy in a black cape shows up, breathing heavy in my ear? I'm shooting first. Han rules. And for the record—" she tapped her Sig against her thigh, "—I'm not doing carbonite."

Will shook his head, but the corner of his mouth twitched.

Behind them, the course stretched in damp silence. Casey kept her eyes on the dark long after Will had turned away.

The board wasn't theirs anymore. Someone else had made the first move.

Kristen's Warning

Clubhouse – Service Hallway (Near Kitchen)

The scent of seared ribeye and garlic butter still clung to the air as Will and Casey cornered Gregory Young just past the swinging service doors. He froze, clutching a crate of glassware to his chest, eyes darting between them.

"Mr. Young," Will said evenly, "we need a word."

Gregory shifted uneasily, his voice low and guarded. "Now? I've got tables—"

"Now," Casey cut him off, arms crossed. She pulled a thin printout from her folder, tapped it once. "Two offshore accounts in the Caymans. Both in your name. You want to explain how a restaurant server pulls that off?"

Gregory's face drained of color. He set the crate down slowly, glass clinking. For a moment, he just rubbed the bridge of his nose, muttering to himself. Then he let out a resigned sigh. "Christ... I knew this was going to bite me."

"Talk," Will said, his tone clipped.

Gregory leaned against the wall, voice cracking with a mix of embarrassment and defensiveness. "It's not what it looks like. My uncle lives in Nassau and runs a fishing charter. When my mom got sick, he fronted money for her treatments. Said the easiest way to keep it clean was to wire it through his bank down there. He set me up with a secondary account so we wouldn't be hit with international fees. I didn't think twice about it. I was trying to keep my mom breathing."

Casey narrowed her eyes. "So you're telling us this isn't cartel money, it's... fishing money?"

Gregory barked a humorless laugh. "Yeah. I'm laundering grouper, Detective. Look, I've got every receipt, every wire statement. IRS has the filings. Hell, check the account balance, you'll see. It's barely enough to cover a decent used car. Nothing dirty about it."

Will studied him for a long moment, silent. Gregory fidgeted under the weight of it, jaw tight, eyes pleading.

Finally, Will spoke, voice low. "You'll send those documents. Today. Every wire, every receipt. If you're lying, we'll know."

"I'm not lying," Gregory said firmly, though his hands still trembled as he shoved them into his apron pockets.

Casey gave a slight shake of her head as she stepped back. "Dead end. He's not our guy."

Will's jaw tightened, but he didn't argue. His eyes shifted past Gregory, out toward the dark stretch of fairway beyond the glass windows. Something cold twisted in his gut. "No," he said quietly.

Will and Casey stepped back into the main corridor, the low hum of dinner service muffled by the thick carpet and paneled walls. The scent of garlic and wine faded behind them, replaced by the faint tang of polish and cigar smoke drifting from the members' lounge.

Casey exhaled hard, shoving her hands into her jacket pockets. "Fishing charters and sick relatives. Not exactly the cartel pipeline I was hoping for."

"Not a lie either," Will muttered, his eyes fixed on the broad glass doors leading to the terrace. Beyond them, the 18th green was a dark sheet of velvet under the moonlight. "If the IRS signed off, he's clean."

They pushed through the doors into the night air. The lake glimmered faintly in the distance, wind carrying the faint lilt of laughter from the bar balcony above. It felt obscene, Will thought, how close the two worlds sat. Death on the greens, cocktails on the terrace.

Casey flicked her gaze across the fairways, scanning shadows by instinct. "We keep circling back to the same board members, the same damn committee, but the threads keep breaking. If this were about money, it's too clean. If it's about revenge, it's too personal. And if it's about power..." She trailed off, her jaw tight.

Will stopped at the edge of the lot, staring across the rolling dark. "Maybe it's all three. Money. Revenge. Control. Somebody still out there thinks the game isn't finished."

Casey kicked at the gravel, eyes narrowing. "So who's keeping score now?"

Neither of them had an answer. The silence between them stretched, filled only by the rustle of pines and the faint, haunting splash of water against the marina docks. Somewhere out in the dark, unseen, the next move was already being planned.

Anderson Home

The house felt too still for the hour. Will had just dropped his keys where he usually does, the familiar clanking signaling that he was home. Kristen came into the living room, her expression caught somewhere between anger and fear. The lamp on the end table cast her in warm light, but her voice was cold.

"This isn't just your case anymore, Will," she said. "It's ours. He's watching all of us. Both girls."

He froze mid-step, scanning her face. Kristen didn't rattle easily, not after Steve, not after the ordeal he put her through. She'd learned how to keep her fear locked behind the DA's composure. But tonight, he could see it bleeding through, in the tightness around her eyes, in the way her hand kept flexing like she wanted to throw something.

"What happened?" Will asked.

Kristen reached to the coffee table, picking up the folded golf scorecard from earlier, the one with her name in red ink, "E/E" scrawled on the back. "We've been acting like this is some puzzle you and Casey can solve if you stare hard enough at the pieces. But every time we turn around, he's closer. He's watching *them*." She set the scorecard down sharply. "And you keep acting like the rest of us are just bystanders in your investigation."

Before Will could answer, a voice cut through from the hallway.

"Good," Ellie said, stepping into view. "Let him watch me."

Kristen spun on her. "What did you just say?"

"I know how to get his attention," Ellie said, chin high, tone daring him to argue. "If he's already following me, why not use it? Make him focus on me, give you a chance to—"

"To *what*?!" Will's voice cracked through the room, sharper than he'd intended. He took a step toward her. "Let him put you on his scoreboard? You still think this is a game you can win with a clever post? Why are you just now showing me this?"

Ellie's jaw tightened. "You and Casey chase him around in the dark, and he still gets the drop on you. At least I can—"

"—stop right there." Casey's voice came from the kitchen doorway. She was leaning against the frame, arms crossed, eyes locked on Ellie. "I like the idea of baiting him," she said, "but it's not gonna be you."

Ellie blinked. "Then who—"

"Me," Casey said flatly. She stepped forward, pulling out her phone. "What's the app you've been using to post all your genius bait?"

Ellie hesitated, then mumbled, "HollowTalk. He DM'd me on there *BookofNumbersV6*. "Good." Casey held out her hand. "Your login info."

Will's head snapped toward her. "Absolutely not—"

But Ellie was already rattling off her username and password. Casey typed them in, and a moment later, her own phone screen lit up with Ellie's feed. "Perfect. I'll log in from my place and talk to him through my laptop. If he can trace an IP, it'll lead him to me, not here." "Of course, you would be using HollowTalk, one of those hard-to-detect apps from a family tracker type of thing, sneaky girl, no wonder your mom didn't know."

Will gave her a look. "You think I'm gonna sign off on you catfishing a serial killer like it's amateur night on *To Catch a Predator*?"

Kristen cut in before Casey could fire back. "I do," she said firmly. "If it keeps him off Ellie's scent and gives you an opening, I'm for it."

Casey smirked at Will. "That's one vote." She tucked the phone away. "I'll keep you in the loop every step. But first, we call Captain Monroe and get him up to speed."

Will didn't like it, every muscle in his body was screaming that this was reckless, but the determined set of Casey's jaw told him the train had already left the station.

Whatever Ellie had just buried in that bag, Emily was starting to think it was part of the same puzzle.

Murphy's Law

Casey's apartment was quiet except for the low hum of her laptop fan. She sat cross-legged on the couch, HollowTalk's login page glowing back at her. Ellie's username and password slid in under her fingers, and seconds later, she was inside, scrolling past photos, rants, and "friends-only" quips Ellie had been dropping for weeks.

"Alright, creep," Casey muttered under her breath, "let's see if you take the bait from me."

She adjusted the profile pic to something grainy and indistinct, wrote a vague, taunting status about "knowing more than I'm saying," and started liking a few of the killer's old coded posts. She didn't expect a response tonight. As she typed out the post, she added a golf emoji almost as an afterthought. "Ellie swore he uses it to flag what matters. Guess we'll see if she was right."

The ping came less than five minutes later.

New private message from: GodBodyCount.

Casey clicked it open and froze. The thumbnail wasn't text. It was a video feed.

Her own living room.

Same couch she was sitting on. Same half-empty coffee mug by her knee. The angle was different, though; it was high, tucked somewhere near the ceiling, pointing straight at her. She looked up, high up on the window; she could see the little red dot flashing on the other side of the transom window, above the drawn shades, Drone! Her mind told her, "What the hell!" Casey screamed, wanting to throw something.

She slammed the laptop shut, heartbeat spiking. Her phone buzzed in her hand before she could even stand up.

A new notification sound and message popped up on HollowTalk.

GodBodyCount: *Have your attention now, Detective?! Didn't kill Gerald McBride. Some One took that away from me. McBride had to pay up for his sins, but not by my hand.*

Casey's skin went cold. Her fingers tightened on the phone until her knuckles hurt.

Two killers. One "Vicar" playing a long game... and someone else with their agenda.

She didn't waste time thinking. She hit Will's contact.

He answered on the first ring. "Casey?"

"He's at my apartment," she said. "Camera drone. Live feed. Watching me while I was on HollowTalk. And Will—" She took a breath. "He says he didn't kill McBride. Someone else did. Somebody who made him pay up first."

Casey continued, "And get this, *GodBodyCount* was the name that Julien used on Steve's dark web service he was using. He's taken over that screenname, Will. How creepy is that?" "

There was a beat of silence on the line before Will spoke again, his voice low and firm. "Then we're not hunting one predator. We're hunting two. Why does it always have to be two? Grab your stuff and meet me at the office. We will get some tech gear and search your apartment later, get out for now."

Casey went to her room to grab her gear and head to the office to meet Will. As she rounded the corner of her bedroom door, something caught her eye, and she froze. Sitting on her pillow was a half-fold scorecard with a familiar logo on the front. The Lakeview at Rocky Pointe Golf Club logo glowed like a beacon in the night.

The scorecard's cover displayed a polished crest: a flagstick on green, crossed irons below, with the lake barely visible in pale blue, a whisper of money and tradition propped up and staring back at her from her bed. The hairs on the back of her neck stood up.

"Why me, this bull shit has to end!" she sighed. She flipped the card over by pulling on her pillow, scrawled on the back, handwritten,

"Bury your face, Grip your pillow tight, Detective – because I'll be the last to rip it." Casey, out loud, said, "Why do they all have to be perverts!" as she snapped a photo with her phone of the writing.

Immediately, Casey grabbed her go bag, hooked her thigh holster waist belt around her, fastened the quick connect buckle, and slid in her trusty Sig Sauer, not taking time to hook it around her leg. Grabbed a few changes of clothes and tossed them in the bag. She picked up her cell phone and slid it into her back pocket, planning to call Will on the way. She ran to the kitchen, grabbed a plastic zipper bag, and then ran back to her bedroom, where she opened it, pushed down on her pillow so the scorecard slid inside, and closed it, and tossed it into her go bag. Grabbed a new toothbrush out of the bathroom sink drawer and tossed it in.

She grabbed her keys off the corner table and headed to the door. Before leaving, she saw her laptop on the couch, grabbed it, tossed it into her computer bag, and strapped it over her shoulder.

Looking around one last time, she let out a breath and looked up at the transom windows by the ceiling for the telltale red light from the drone camera. It was gone.

Casey opened the door, and as she reached back to grab it, she knocked it further open with her bag. "Ugggh!" she groaned. She stepped back to grab the handle and pull it, and as she stepped back out, she tripped over the threshold and almost fell. "Damn it! Not my day." Reaching into her pocket to get the key to lock the deadbolt, she dropped her keys. Casey let out a long, "Really!" Leaning over to pick them up, Casey gets slammed from behind, propelling her into the half-open door, bags, and her assailant back into the doorway.

The world jolted. Her chest slammed into the half-open door. The edge bit her ribs. Bags tangled across her shoulder, weight jerking her sideways. The force of the assailant drove her deeper into the frame, flesh and wood colliding.

Instinct roared through her. *Get up. Get free.*

She rolled, fought to get her arm under her, but the strap pinned her tight. The assailant stuck to her, legs wrapped around her to control her. The pistol in her thigh holster might as well have been a mile away.

Then the arm came around. Heavy. Squeezing. Rear choke hold, perfect textbook.

Casey's pulse spiked. She knew that grip. Knew it too well.

Cain. Rogers. The night they kicked me, threw me around, and dragged me under, choking me out like a rag doll. Cain later told me, calmly and clinically, how they planned to take turns. Pose me. White paint. Public spectacle. Will's sirens saved me then. Just barely.

The smell hit.

Sweet. Chemical. Rotten-sweet. Chloroform.

Her brain screamed. *Not this time.*

She drove her elbow back, heels slamming down, body thrashing. Every ounce of muscle fought to keep air in her lungs.

"Not this time!" she snarled, voice raw.

Her hand found the grip at her thigh. The Sig was there. Solid. Familiar. The beavertail tang pressed into the web of her palm, grounding her. *Yes. Weapon. Power.*

Her thumb slid the release. She drew it, raising the barrel blind, angling it up toward the weight crushing her.

Shoot. Don't hesitate.

But the dark was already edging her vision, tunneling. The chloroform dragged her under, merciless.

Her finger tightened—

A hand snapped around her wrist, vice-strong. Twisted. Slammed her hand down as the Sig wrenched free, clattering to the floor.

No, no, no.

Her world narrowed. The smell filled her skull. Blackness swallowed everything.

Her last thought flared sharp as a blade: *I will not die like this.*

Casey's Apartment Floor

Casey woke up lying on her back. Not knowing how long she was out, she could tell she was resting on her hands. "Oh great, here we go again," she thought. She could feel the cold floor against her bare shoulders. When she tried to see how tightly her hands were restrained, they moved as she pulled; they slid out from under her. "What in the hell?" she said out loud.

She rolled over to all fours, realizing she no longer had her shirt, but her pants and holster were still intact. She glanced around the room and saw her pistol on the floor and scurried over to pick it up.

Jumping up to one knee with the pistol out at the ready, she scanned the apartment. She did a quick scan of herself since she saw some blood on her forearm, for injuries, she couldn't find any, then she smelled that familiar metallic smell as a drop of blood curled across her lip and onto her chest. With her senses starting to catch up with her, Casey looked down and realized that she was still wearing her bra, noticing the blood from her nose had been dripping for some time, and she was just now seeing its telltale sign.

On a chair that appeared to have been pulled out from her table in the kitchen area was a department-embroidered polo shirt, which had been cut to shreds and left draped over the back of the chair. The chair was positioned as if whoever attacked her was sitting in it, watching her lie on the floor.

"Ok, Fox Mulder, I need you about right now," Casey said out loud. She stood up and swept the rest of her apartment for her attacker. Empty, every room. Whoever it was had attacked her, obviously didn't kill her, but stripped her of her shirt, and left one of her department polos sliced to shreds, staged on a chair.

She went to the bathroom, pulled some tissue from the roll, and shoved it against her nose as she squeezed it to try to stop the bleeding. Within a few minutes, it had finally given up the outpour she was dealing with when she had awakened. She took off her now bloodstained bra, tossing it into the sink.

She went to her dresser, retrieved a clean one, and put it on, followed by a department polo shirt from the closet. Leaving her closet, she realized that one of her drawers was still partially open on her dresser. As she got closer, she realized that it wasn't the drawer she kept her bras in that she had just opened, but the one below it, where she kept her underwear. She could see that it looked empty. As she started to shut it, she could see the black felt that lined the bottom of the drawer. Totally empty. "What in the world is this shit?" Casey barked. But inside, whoever took her underwear left her something in return. A handwritten note:

Lace is all I took. Next time it'll be you.

Casey now totally freaked out like she had never been before, ran to the kitchen, grabbed her go bag, her laptop bag, keys, and bolted out the door, gun in hand. She ran straight for her car. She tossed her bags inside and realized she had left her phone behind. Casey just hopped in and drove to the precinct to find Will. She needed someone that she could trust, someone that had her back no matter what.

Back at the Office

By the time Casey reached the precinct, Will was already in the conference room, the board lit with crime scene photos and a timeline of the killings. McBride's ballroom photo sat in the middle like an uninvited guest at the table.

"I knew the McBride scene was off, been reviewing it in my mind even before today," Will said before she even sat down. His voice was flat, certain. "Wrong staging. No sermon verse. No golf glove. And the wine paint? Too bright. Too fresh. Our guy doesn't rush."

Casey had not said a word, and she let out a slow, quiet, direct, "Will."

Will spun around immediately, knowing that something was wrong, something was wrong with his partner.

She had her go-bag slung over one shoulder, her laptop case in the other, and a look that made his stomach knot.

"Casey." He crossed the room fast, pulse spiking. She looked pale, her hair askew, and for a terrifying split second, he thought she'd been shot. "What the hell happened?"

She dropped the bags at his feet with a thud. "You want the short version or the part where I almost got strangled in my own doorway?"

Will's jaw locked so tight it ached. "Start at the beginning."

Casey blew out a sharp breath and leaned against the edge of the conference room table, arms folded tight. "As soon as I hung up with you, I went to grab my gear. Walked into my bedroom, and there it was—on my pillow. A Rocky Pointe scorecard, like it was waiting for me. You know the logo, with its neat little flag and crossed irons. Turned it over and in big red letters: '

Bury your face, grip your pillow tight, Detective, because I'll be the last to rip it.'"

Will felt his stomach twist. The words crawled under his skin like rot. He kept his voice even. "You touched it?"

"Bagged it in plastic. Evidence. But that's when things went sideways. I grabbed my gear and went for the door. Before I could lock it, somebody slammed me from behind. Shoved me into the frame hard enough to see stars. Arm locked around my throat, chloroform rag in my face."

Her tone was steady, but Will caught the flicker in her eyes. He hated it, hated that she had to relive it.

"I fought," she continued. "Got my Sig out, safety off, finger on the damn trigger. But whoever it was, they had the advantage with the sedative. Grabbed my wrist before I could fire. Next thing I know, lights out."

Will's hands curled into fists at his sides, nails biting his palms. He saw it too vividly: her going limp, dragged like prey. And the sick fear hit him again, the memory of the last time he'd almost lost her.

"How long were you under?" he asked, his voice lower now.

"No idea." She shook her head. "When I came to, I was on my back. Nose bleeding, shirt gone. One of my department polos was shredded and staged across a chair like some freak show centerpiece, as if he had been watching me from it. I go into the bedroom, my drawer left open, and find all my underwear gone. Think they tried some of my perfume as well, and I could smell it lingering." Her gaze locked on his. "And a note left behind: *'Lace is all I took. Next time it'll be you.'*"

The words landed like a punch. For a moment, Will couldn't breathe. They could have killed her. They should have killed her. Instead, they wanted her rattled. Marked. His mind raced to every crime scene where bodies were displayed for shock value, every family gutted to make a point. "They could have killed you," he let out.

Casey didn't flinch. "That's the point. They didn't. This wasn't about killing me. It was about control—getting inside my head. And yeah, they rattled me." She lifted her chin, defiant. "But I'm still standing. And I'm done letting them call the shots."

Will exhaled slowly, every instinct screaming to grab her, to hold her still and safe. Instead, he forced calm into his voice. "Then we play it smart. We lock this down. Whoever put their hands on you left a trail, and I'll find it."

Casey's smirk was faint, bitter around the edges. "Damn right you will. Because next time, I'm not blacking out, I'm putting two in their chest."

Will didn't answer right away. The bullpen felt too crowded, too many eyes watching, pretending not to listen. He reached down, scooped up her go-bag, and jerked his chin toward the hallway.

"Come with me."

Casey frowned. "What—"

"Now," he said, the word clipped.

They walked in silence down the corridor until he pushed open the door to the stairwell. The echo of their boots on the concrete replaced the low hum of the precinct. The door swung shut behind them, sealing them off.

Will set her bag on the step and turned to face her. His jaw worked, like the words he wanted to say were too jagged to get out clean. Finally, his voice came low and rough.

"You could've been dead when I got that call. Do you understand that? Dead, Casey."

Her expression softened, but she didn't back down. "But I'm not. I'm here."

"That's not the point." His hand raked through his hair. "He was in your apartment. Sitting in a chair and watching you. You don't walk away from that. Not twice. Not without scars."

Casey's chin lifted, stubborn as ever. "I've had scars since before you knew my name. And yeah, he rattled me, but he didn't finish the job. That means he wanted me alive, and that's his mistake."

Will stepped closer, close enough that she could see the strain in his eyes, the raw edge of something he usually buried deep. "You joke about it, you make your Star Wars cracks, but this isn't a game. You think I can stand another body staged on a floor, yours, and keep going?"

Her breath caught, just for a second.

"Will—"

He cut her off. "No. Listen. We stop him before he gets another chance. You don't go anywhere alone. Not home, not a store run, not even for coffee. Not until this bastard's in the ground."

Casey crossed her arms, her usual shield. But her voice was quieter now. "You're scared. I get it. But don't you dare sideline me. If I back off now, he wins."

He exhaled hard through his nose, the fight between logic and fear etched across his face. He finally nodded once. "Fine. But from here on out, you and me, we move together. No more almosts."

For a long moment, the stairwell was silent but for the hum of the building. Casey tilted her head, a shadow of a grin returning. "You know, Anderson, you're a lot more intense when you're worried about me."

Will's mouth twitched, but his voice stayed flat. "Don't get used to it."

She smirked, grabbed her bag from the step, and swung it over her shoulder. "Too late."

Will followed her out of the stairwell, the tight coil in his chest still wound, but now bound by resolve. Whoever had touched her, whoever thought they could get away with leaving her alive, had just signed their own death warrant.

Back in the Conference Room

Will got them both a cup of coffee and returned to the conference room. Casey dropped her bag on the table, picked up the coffee, took a big sip, and let out a breath. "You know how you were saying you thought the McBride scene was off. Well, as I mentioned on the phone, the chatroom user using Steve's old screen name claimed he didn't do McBride. "

Will's gaze sharpened. "The Vicar told you that?"

"He sent me a private message on HollowTalk, right after I'd been building the fake persona. It was a live feed from a hidden camera in my apartment, a drone positioned to look through the top windows over my blinds. And then he said McBride had to pay up, that someone else took him out. He sounded pissed. Not like he was bluffing."

Will looked back at McBride's crime scene photo, jaw tightening. "So he lost a mark. Somebody beat him to it."

"Exactly," Casey said, leaning over the table to trace the sequence of murders with her finger. "The Vicar's list is still clean, Whitmore, Gilmore, Yates the chapel vic, all tied to the toxic waste cover-up. McBride? He was on our list, but what was the reason he was killed before the Vicar could? What's the connection... unless you count owing money to someone in the laundering network."

Will's expression darkened. "Which means we've got two hunters. The Vicar, meticulous, working his list, and someone else, picking off targets for a different reason."

Casey smirked faintly, trying to cut the tension. "Double the fun."

Will gave her a look. "Double the variables."

She grinned anyway. "And here you said you were getting too old for this shit."

"Don't start."

"Okay, Sergeant Murtaugh," she teased, straightening.

Will shook his head but allowed the slightest flicker of a smile. "Let's pull Price's financials. If McBride was paying someone off, it's in the money trail."

"Oh, by the way," Casey added, "I don't have my phone, it's either at the house or he took it while he was drooling over me half naked on the floor of my apartment. I took photos of the scorecard and my drawer."

"We will go look to see if we need to get you a new one. Can you lock it remotely from your computer?" Will interjected.

"I'll see what I can do." She said, "Damn it, man." Holding her hands out in frustration.

"What? What is it?" Will returned.

"Do you know how much money I have spent on underwear, and how much that drawer was worth? Replacing it all is going to be a bitch, I'm glad I tossed a pair in my bag before I left," Casey groaned, jumping up to check her go bag, "Yeah, Sith Lord missed one."

Casey caught a glimpse of Kristen in the hallway outside the interview rooms, crossing through the hallway connector to the courthouse. She still had her coat on, her hair pulled back, one hand wrapped around a coffee as if it was holding her together. Catching up to her.

"Got a second?" Casey asked.

Kristen gave her a wary look. "You've got that face."

"This isn't a formal briefing," Casey said, lowering her voice. "Just... you should know. The Vicar's got eyes inside my apartment. Sent me a live feed. And—" she hesitated, "—he says he didn't kill McBride. Someone else did."

Casey whispers, *"I was attacked inside my apartment as a message for them, trying to scare me. I'm OK, before you start. I have your overlord, protector, husband, standing guard over me now."*

Kristen's grip on her coffee tightened until her knuckles whitened. "Two of them?"

"Not in the apartment, but two killers, operating separately from each other, not together. But it seems that way. Will always said the McBride scene felt wrong. Now we understand why." Casey's tone softened. "I told Will immediately. But I wanted you to hear it from me because if The Vicar can see me, there's no telling who else he's watching. You and the girls need to lock things down tighter than ever.

Kristen nodded slowly, but her jaw tightened in that familiar way, the one that indicated she wasn't going to sit back and hide. "We'll handle it. But you tell me if there's even a whisper of him looking our way again."

Casey smirked faintly. "Promise. And Kristen—" she leaned in a little, "You're my girl, and with how my day has been, I don't want to be on bad terms with Ellie right now, even after I scared her the other day. I'm sorry that you had to deal with the fallout from her."

Kristen's expression softened just enough to let some warmth show. "You don't owe me an apology, Casey. Like I said back at the house, she should know you love her, even if you have a messed-up way of showing it sometimes."

Casey grinned. "Messed-up's my brand."

Down the hall, Will appeared from the conference room, holding a fresh printout. "Price's accounts are dirty as hell," he said, striding over. "Cartel charity tournament is dirty."

Kristen shot Casey a knowing look before heading for the elevator. Casey fell into step beside Will.

"So now we're juggling two killers and an international laundering op," she said. "You still think you're just too old for this shit, or should I get you that rocking chair?"

Will groaned, but she caught the corner of his mouth twitch. "No chair, maybe a new Beretta."

A Second Hunter

Kristen hated the way the late sun pooled across the cul-de-sac, too orange, too thin, like it was bleeding out. She pulled into the driveway, killed the engine, and sat for a moment longer than necessary. The house looked calm enough, porch light off, blinds half-drawn, but her gut itched in that way it had ever since Steve.

She gathered her files, slung her bag over her shoulder, and stepped out. That's when she saw it.

A car. Black sedan. Parked three houses down at the curb. Windows tinted darker than state law allowed.

No neighbor owned that car. She would have known.

Kristen pretended not to notice, but her pulse quickened as she moved toward the front door. A glance over her shoulder: no movement. No flicker of a phone screen. Just an idle machine sitting too still.

Inside, she set her files on the counter, but didn't take off her coat. She slipped to the front window and eased the curtain back with one finger. The car was still there. Engine on now, a faint purr she could feel more than hear.

She dialed Will. He didn't answer; it went straight to voicemail.

Casey's number next. This time, she picked up on the first ring. "Tell me it's about Moscato."

Kristen's voice was tight. "No. Someone's watching the house."

The silence on the line sharpened. "The Vicar?"

Kristen shook her head, eyes locked on the still car. "No. Wrong feel. He likes theater. This is… business. Clean. Quiet."

The sedan idled for another ten seconds, then eased away from the curb. No rush. No screech of tires. Just a slow, deliberate departure, as if to say: I was here. Remember it.

Kristen's stomach clenched. She knew that kind of message. Courtroom witnesses had described it to her too many times, the way cartel shadows made themselves known without ever stepping into the light.

Casey's voice cut back in, clipped and serious now. "Get the plate?"

"Too far," Kristen said. "But I saw the sticker on the bumper. Marina permit. Lakeview docks."

Casey swore softly. "That's not his style. That's someone else's play. Maybe someone is tying off loose ends."

Kristen let the curtain fall back into place, the room suddenly too dim. "So we've got two hunters circling the same board."

"And neither cares about the rules," Casey muttered. "Stay inside. Lock up. I'll send a unit to cruise by the house."

Kristen hung up, her breath shallow. Upstairs, she could hear the girls moving, Emily humming, Ellie's door slamming. Normal life echoing through a house already marked.

But in her bones, Kristen felt it: tonight wasn't The Vicar. Tonight was something colder. A different predator had come to take measure of her.

And predators didn't visit without a reason.

Kristen let the curtain fall back into place. The sedan was gone, but its absence felt worse than its presence. A ghost car, leaving only pressure in her chest.

She double-checked the locks, then sat at the kitchen table with her phone still clutched in her hand. Casey stayed on the line.

"You sure you're good till we swing by?" Casey asked.

Kristen's eyes tracked the empty driveway. "I'll sit tight. The house is locked. Lights on. Girls are upstairs. ... get here fast."

Casey's voice softened, just a hair. "We're moving."

The call ended. Kristen set the phone down but didn't let go. She stayed at the table, waiting for the sound of Will's boots on the porch or Casey's laugh at the door.

Outside, the night pressed close, too quiet. Kristen's pulse ticked the seconds louder than the clock.

An Unwanted Piece

The board is mine. Every square, every file, every rank, I have measured them.

And yet tonight, a shadow parks itself at the edge of the game, idling in silence. Not mine. Not the Vicar's.

An intruder piece. No grace, no scripture, no patience. It does not stalk. It does not test. It waits with headlights dim, a rook of iron and smoke with two pawns, but not my Rook. This one belongs to a different player, one who plays without boards, without moves, a player who erases rather than advances.

Cartel. I know the scent of their money. The way their hunters circle. They are not artists. They are janitors. Cleaners.

And cleaners are dangerous because they do not care who is swept into the fire.

Already, they burn the evidence of their missteps. Already, they send their warning in smoke.

I close my eyes and see the marina, wood slick with oil, rope blackening in flame, a boat collapsing into itself. Not an accident. A message. The board lit at its edge.

The others will think the blaze is chaotic, random, and tragic.

I know better.

It is an intrusion. A second hand reaching onto my board.

But two players cannot rule the same match. One must yield.

And I have never yielded.

The Marina Dead End

The SUV hummed down Lakeview Road, fog ghosting across the ditches. Will had one hand on the wheel, the other working the radio.

"Unit 11-Baker, this is Thirteen David. Have you swung by the Anderson house yet?" Casey asked.

Static crackled before a woman's voice came back, smooth with a Carolina drawl but steady as a seasoned pro. "Copy that. I rolled past twice. The house looks as if it is locked up tight. Lights on, no movement outside except one vehicle."

Will's eyes flicked to Casey. "Vehicle?"

"Did you say vehicle? Get a Description?" Casey questioned.

Officer Savanna Jo Coltrane continued, "Black SUV. Saw it parked three houses down. When I turned onto the street, it pulled off slowly, like it knew I was coming. Couldn't get close enough to snag a plate before it disappeared into the fog."

Casey leaned into the mic. "What'd you catch?"

"Just the reflective sticker," Coltrane replied. "Marina permit. Lakeview docks. That yellow and red stuck out like a sore thumb."

Casey whistled low. "Sharp eyes, Jo."

Savanna Jo chirped back, "Sharp eyes aren't optional. They're survival."

Will cracked the faintest smile, then keyed the mic. "Good work. Stay sharp tonight."

"Always do," Coltrane said, signing off.

Casey shook her head with a half-grin. "Farm girl instincts and a badge. She doesn't miss much. If Jo says it peeled off to the marina, I'd bet my paycheck on it."

Before Will could answer, his phone lit with a vibrating buzz on the console. Priority dispatch. He glanced at the screen, then at Casey.

"Boat fire at the club's marina," he said. "Witness says somebody was pouring gas before it went up."

Casey's brows shot up. "That's subtle."

Will hit the turn signal, swinging them toward the lake road. "It's not subtle. It's a message. A swift one."

Casey muttered, buckling tighter, "And here I thought our night was already full."

By the time Will and Casey reached the marina, the night air was heavy with the acrid tang of burned fiberglass and scorched varnish. Red strobes from fire trucks bounced across the water, making the ripples look like fiery shards of broken glass.

At the tape, Officer Savanna Jo Coltrane was already posted. Ball cap pulled low, blonde hair spilling out the back, her patrol jacket snug over long legs and scuffed boots. She had one hand steadying a jittery dockhand while jotting notes with the other.

Jo spotted them first, tipping her chin. "Detectives. You took your time."

Casey ducked under the tape with a smirk. "Some of us don't have the luxury of hiding cover-girl looks under a ball cap. Some of us have to earn our charm the hard way."

Jo's grin was quick and cutting. "Oh, don't sell yourself short. Cute redhead, sure... though right now you look like somebody used your face as a speed bag. Hope he was worth it."

Casey's brows shot up, but her smile only widened. "Oh, I like you."

Will brushed past both of them, gravel crunching under his boots. "Focus. What've we got?"

Jo flipped her notepad. "Witnesses say a man in a dark hoodie was pouring gas on that sailboat before it went up. Tall, moved like he knew he was being watched. Walked off before the fire caught."

She nodded toward the charred husk still hissing at the dock. A half-melted nameplate dangled from the stern, letters warped but legible: **Sea's the Day.**

Casey let out a low whistle. "So, arson in full view. Not even pretending it was an accident."

Before Jo could reply, a man in a security jacket jogged over from the shack at the end of the pier. He was sweating, his skin faintly smelling of smoke and nerves.

"Detectives? Officer Coltrane told me to check our feeds soon as I got here." He glanced between them. "Most of the system's down for maintenance, but one camera was live—the fuel dock lens. She figured it might've caught something."

Jo gave a little shrug, tucking her notepad into her pocket. "Lucky guess."

Casey's gaze flicked to her, grudging respect breaking through the smirk. "Sharp eyes. Not bad for a farm girl."

Savanna Jo's mouth curved. "Back home, noticing the little things kept the cows in and the coyotes out." Will cut them off with a nod toward the shack. "Show us."

The guard led them inside. The air was damp from the fire hoses, monitors humming in a dim glow. Most screens were dark, but one feed blinked in the corner.

He tapped the keyboard. "This is all we got."

The footage stuttered to life, grainy and slightly out of focus. A figure in a dark hoodie walked the length of the pier, a gas can swinging loose at his side. He moved like a man who expected to be seen. No rush, no panic.

Will leaned closer, eyes narrowing. "He wanted us to have this."

The figure paused mid-pier, head turning just enough to catch the camera's lens flare. For half a second, the hood shadow shifted—no face, not clear, but deliberate. Then he bent, poured a long line of liquid across the deck, and struck a match.

The screen flared white as the fire burst into flames. When the static cleared, the pier was empty.

Casey blew out a sharp breath. "Well. That's not The Vicar's style. He's showy, but he's careful. This? This is theater."

"Cartel theater," Will said, eyes still locked on the frozen image. The hooded figure's outline lingered on the screen, burned in like an afterimage. "They're not hiding their hand. They're reminding us that not one but two games are being played."

Casey folded her arms. "And if we keep chasing one, the other's going to cut our legs out from under us."

Will finally looked away from the monitor, the reflection of fire still etched in his gaze. "Then we split the board. One killer, one cartel. And hope the lines don't cross before we're ready."

The guard hovered nearby, uneasy. "So what do I put in the report, Detective?"

Will's voice was flat, leaving no room for doubt. "Arson. Intentional. And tell your captain: this wasn't a fire. It was a warning. I need a copy of this footage, from the hour before until we arrived."

Watcher's Journal — Flames on the File

The board shifts under smoke.

One fire on the water, and the pawns panic. They believe the match has begun. They do not see this as only an opening gambit.

A rook from another board intruded tonight. Cartel men, heavy-handed and graceless, stumbling across squares that were never theirs.

They do not understand the rules. They do not respect the game.

Left alone, they would foul every pattern, scatter every move.

So they were removed.

Pieces like that deserve no strategy, no mercy. Their erasure was necessary... and satisfying.

The Vicar dresses his moves in scripture, cloaking blood with sermons and ritual.

But I do not play with verses.

I keep the board clean.

Where he gilds death with prophecy, I reduce it to silence.

The Knight bristles at the flames, leaping at ghosts, restless as ever. He is quick, clever, and brave, but too eager to guard squares already gone.

The Queen prowls at home with her pawns, her voice sharp enough to cut glass. She cannot resist an open challenge; queens never do. Her pawns move because she wills it, though they do not yet understand the power of their place. Two girls, fragile and fierce both, waiting to be tested.

But it is the Rook I watch.

She does not fear smoke. She does not blink at fire. She drives forward, blunt and unstoppable, and the board trembles when she moves.

Rooks are not meant to matter this much in the opening. Yet this one does. She shatters patterns. She ruins careful plans. She is the only piece I cannot predict.

And if she smashes my game before I am ready, there will be no endgame at all.

So I wait.

The fire consumes.

And I keep my silence.

Smoke on the Water

By the time the flames were out, the smell of charred fiberglass still clung to the marina like a wet tarp. Firefighters rolled hoses, their lights painting the water in stuttering red and white, reflections warping with every ripple.

Will and Casey stepped past the tape, boots thudding on damp planks. Uniforms clustered at the end of the dock, and a coroner's van backed in with its doors yawning open.

Officer Savanna Jo Coltrane met them there, ball cap pulled low, notepad in hand, face grim in the flashing lights. "Two bodies on board," she said. "Too burned for immediate ID. Male, both of them. From the size, I'd call it mid-forties to fifties."

Casey swore under her breath. "So this wasn't just a message. Somebody was cleaning house."

Jo gave a curt nod. "Boat's registered to Jack Smith—McBride's old law partner. Retired after McBride stepped away, but word was he still had his fingers in things. Cartel ties whispered about for years. Never proven."

Will's jaw flexed, his voice flat. "Then they weren't random. They were meant to go up with the ship."

The hiss of cooling wreckage filled the silence. Casey's gaze drifted over the black water lapping at the pilings. "Cartel sending signals. First a fire, now bodies. Next step?

Henchmen. Muscle on the ground to make sure no more leaks spring."

Will didn't answer, but the heaviness in his silence spoke enough.

Jo closed her notebook with a snap. "Whatever this is, it's not going away quietly."

Casey gave her a sidelong glance. "You don't rattle easily, do you?"

Jo's mouth curved. "Neither do you."

Casey let out a short breath, almost a laugh. "Guess we've both been in worse places."

Jo's eyes lingered on her, steady. "Yeah. And we're both still standing."

For a moment, the red and white strobes painted them in the same hard light, two different kinds of survivors sizing each other up.

Will broke the silence, voice cutting through. "Focus. We've got more to lose if this keeps spreading."

An Hour Later – Precinct AV Room

The glow of monitors bathed the room in blue. The tech scrubbed through minutes of dockside footage, most of it dull: fishermen dragging coolers, dockhands hauling lines. Then, a flicker of color made Will sit forward sharply.

"Pause. Zoom in."

The operator froze the frame, enlarging a section of the pier. Bright blue sneakers glowed under the sodium lights, the exact shade Will had seen on Ellie's feet more times than he could count.

Casey's breath hissed out. "Tell me that's not her."

Will's pulse thudded in his ears. He leaned closer, as if proximity might change the image. Ellie's height. Ellie's posture.

Then, in the next frame, just behind her shoulder, blurred but unmistakable, the hooded figure. The same narrow-shouldered silhouette they'd seen haunting the perimeter near the fairway.

Casey's voice dropped, steady but taut. "That's the clearest shot of him we've got yet."

Will didn't answer. His chest felt hollow. All he could see was how close she'd been, one step, one breath away from a killer. His mind already spun ahead, past evidence, past suspects. To Kristen. To Ellie. To the conversation, he'd have to survive with both.

Because this wasn't a warning anymore, it was proof.

The fire had burned two men to ash, but its smoke carried another message entirely: Ellie wasn't just bait. She was already in the crosshairs.

Watcher's Journal — Burned Pawns

The board trembles when fire takes the edge.

Tonight, two rooks were sacrificed, not mine, not the Vicar's. Cartel pawns. Burned where they stood, crude pieces removed with gasoline and smoke. That is how their masters play: blunt, graceless, preferring to scorch the board rather than maneuver. A message written in flame instead of moves.

But flame spreads. Smoke hides. Even a rook on fire casts its shadow across the squares. And in that shadow, other pieces stumble closer.

The Knight came first, drawn by duty, heavy with questions. The Rook beside him, restless, her fury sharp as glass. They think they stand against the blaze.

But it was the forward Pawn who wandered nearest the flame. Bright shoes flashing, eyes fixed on horizons she cannot see. Pawns crave the open file, even when it is already threatened. They do not sense the jaws until the capture is certain. She does not know how close she strayed to the noose.

And still... the Rook. She stalked the pier with eyes that swept too far, too fast, as if she might catch my reflection in the water. She has not yet grasped her danger, but I have grasped hers. Rooks may be blunt, but they smash holes in neat strategies, and the board shivers every time she rolls forward.

The cartel believes it controls the fire. The Vicar believes he controls the sermon.

But I alone watch the true game.

And the Pawn does not yet see the square she occupies has already been marked.

Will is Not Thrilled

Kristen was halfway through rinsing a mug when Will's voice came from the doorway, low, sharp, and unmistakably pissed.

"Want to tell me why your sneakers were on the dock at the marina thirty minutes before a boat went up in flames?"

Ellie froze halfway down the hall. "What?"

Casey was leaning against the counter, arms crossed, watching. "Bright blue Hokas, white letters. Hard to miss on security footage. You were there."

"I was just hanging out with friends, we were making TikTok videos, you told me not to be alone," Ellie said, too fast. "We weren't anywhere near—" "Don't," Will cut in, stepping closer.

"The footage also shows a man, the same height and build as our suspect, in the background. So you weren't just hanging out in some safe little bubble. You were within fifty feet of him."

Kristen's hand tightened on the mug. "Ellie..." "I didn't know he was there! We were just having fun." Ellie shot back, but her voice cracked.

Will's jaw flexed. "That's the problem. You don't know. And you've been treating this like a game."

Emily looked between them. "Wait, are you saying that guy was The Vicar?"

Casey shook her head. "Not necessarily. That's the other thing. We've been holding back something until we were sure." She set her phone on the counter, screen dark but heavy in her hand. "*GodBodyCount*, the account tied to The Vicar, sent me a message through HollowTalk. Hidden camera footage from inside my apartment. He wanted me to know he's been there. And then he said something else..."

Will took it from there. "He told her he didn't kill Gerald McBride."

Kristen frowned. "That's what Casey was saying earlier. Then who did?"

"That's the point," Casey said. "Someone else. Someone who made it look like it might be The Vicar, but the scene was all wrong, no paint, no verse, none of his staging. Will saw it from the jump."

"I knew the McBride scene was off," Will said, leaning against the island. "This just confirmed it. McBride 'had to pay up,' according to him. No sermon. No scripture. Just dead."

Emily's eyes narrowed. "So there's a second killer."

"Exactly," Will said. "Two different predators in play. One's the Vicar, the other's still a question mark. And both now know exactly who you are."

Ellie shifted under the weight of his stare. "So... what happens now?"

Casey's voice was steady. "Now you lock down your online footprint. No more breadcrumbs, no more location tags, nothing that lets either of them track you. The Vicar's already used your posts once. We're not giving him or anyone else another shot."

Will's gaze swept from Ellie to Emily to Kristen. "This isn't a suggestion. No more solo walks, no more fence-hopping, no more meeting up with friends without telling one of us exactly where you'll be. Understand?"

Kristen gave a single, tight nod. "We understand."

The silence that followed wasn't just agreement, it was the unspoken realization that this was no longer Will's case alone. The hunt had moved straight into their home.

Casey looked at Will and said, "Come on, we still have some killers to catch." And they set off into the setting sun to the police department, eager to catch a killer.

Girl in the Video

Casey's phone buzzed with the Cybercrimes tag, *URGENT — PRIORITY FILE.* She slid into an empty conference room before Will could ask, locking the door behind her. The laptop glowed as the file unspooled.

At first it looked like one of Ellie's posts, same cheer jacket, same trail gear, same quick grin before the lens. Then the frame jolted, blurred, and the video twisted into something else.

Ellie, shoved from behind.

Ellie, dragged across wet grass, her phone tumbling out of frame.

Ellie, screaming, hand over her mouth.

Casey's throat tightened. She scrubbed back. Frame by frame. Something was off. The shadows didn't line up, the mouths moved half a beat late, the hands blurred into nothing if she paused long enough. Not real.

But spliced.

Stolen.

Pieced together from her actual feed, and from angles that shouldn't exist.

The final image froze on Ellie's face, eyes wide with terror, mouth open in a soundless scream. Then text burned across the screen in red:

"Pawn Taken."

Casey slammed the lid shut, pulse pounding.

Her radio chirped. "Anderson? You copy?"

"Copy," she rasped, forcing her voice flat. "Cybercrimes just confirmed, this wasn't posted to any forum. It was sent directly to me. Meaning he's inside our channel."

Silence stretched for a beat before the voice came back. "What do you want us to tell Will?"

Casey rubbed her temples. Will could not see that video, not yet. Not with the way he'd been staring at Ellie like she was already halfway gone.

"Nothing," she said at last. "Not until we know how deep this breach goes."

Still, when she shut her eyes, the frozen image burned in her mind, Ellie's face, twisted in terror that wasn't hers. Not yet.

"He is toying with the wrong family," Casey muttered. Then, under her breath, a sharper edge: "And if he thinks he's the Emperor, he's about to find out this isn't his Death Star."

She gave a humorless snort, shaking her head. "Mulder would say *the truth is out there.* Sure. But I'd rather put two rounds in it when I find it."

Watcher's Journal — Isolating the Rook

The board is nearly stripped. Fewer pieces now, fewer distractions. The file is open, the ranks thinning. The endgame approaches.

And still, the Rook moves.

She crashes through my lines, shielding pawns that should have fallen already.

She draws the Queen from her corners, forces the King to move when he would rather stay still.

The Pawns trust her shadow more than their own blood.

But I know the truth.

Rooks shine brightest when the board empties. They stretch their reach, they carve the longest lines, and for a moment, they look unstoppable. But that reach betrays them. Too far, too exposed, too eager to smash through the silence.

Rooks always believe they are untouchable.

Rooks forget they cannot move backward.

So I strip away her cover. I cut her lines. I open the board so wide that her power becomes her prison.

She thinks herself the hammer.

But soon she will learn she is the nail.

The Rook stands alone now, isolated from her King and Pawns, too deep on the file to retreat.

I have waited for this moment.

The Rook has one more move left. And I already know where she will fall.

Later – Anderson House

The house settled into uneasy quiet. Upstairs, Emily and Ellie's room hummed with the glow of their laptops, muffled voices drifting through the walls as they debated posts and profiles.

Will and Casey were still back at the precinct, combing through the marina footage frame by frame.

Downstairs, Kristen moved quietly through the rooms, gathering case files from the dining table, her phone still in her other hand. The house seemed to breathe with her, creaks in the walls, the faint hum of the fridge, the rhythmic ticking of the clock.

At the back door, she paused, keys dangling loosely in her hand. Outside, the motion light snapped on, flooding the deck with sterile white. For a moment, it caught nothing but shadows, tree branches bowing in the wind, the grass bending in restless waves.

A flash of lightning rippled across the far sky, distant but bright, a reminder of how storms sometimes rolled in without warning in the Carolina summer.

Kristen sighed, spotting her SUV in the driveway, windows still cracked halfway down. She muttered under her breath, something about bad habits, and slipped out into the night.

At the same time, Ellie came down the stairs, her phone lighting her face in pale blue. She slowed when she saw her mom heading toward the Tahoe. The air felt heavy, charged, the kind that made the hair on your arms rise. Another flash lit the yard, thunder rumbling closer this time.

Kristen had her hand on the driver's door when Ellie stepped out after her. "Mom, I'll get it," she said. "I think I left the back window down earlier."

The two of them crossed paths in the drive, lightning flashing again as the wind picked up, rattling the trees and carrying with it the odd groan of shifting wood, fence? deck? It was impossible to tell.

Kristen frowned, glancing toward the tree line. "Storm's moving in fast," she murmured. "Let's just roll them up and head back inside."

Another creak echoed through the dark, louder this time, metal straining against metal, but it blended with the crash of thunder. The kind of sound you'd second-guess once you were safe inside.

Ellie tugged open the passenger door. Kristen moved to the driver's side. The dome light blinked on, then off as both doors shut.

And then the night swallowed everything again.

The wind pressed harder, shaking the branches, masking the low thud of a door shutting firmly. A moment later, the motion light clicked off, leaving the driveway in shadow.

The Tahoe sat still in the dark, its glossy surface catching one more flicker of lightning before the storm rolled closer.

Inside the house, Emily looked up from her laptop at the faint sound of thunder. For a second, she thought she heard a car door, maybe even tires crunching gravel. She tilted her head toward the window, listening.

But the night had already gone quiet again.

The Radio Call

A call jolted Will from his desk before dawn. Static over the line, then a uniform's voice, urgent, ragged with the kind of tone every cop recognizes: "Detective, we've got an abandoned vehicle. SUV on the ninth fairway, lights still on. Registration comes back to Will and Kristen Anderson, your address."

The words hit like a hammer. For a split second, the room tilted, the edges of Will's vision tunneling. His chair screeched back as he was on his feet, phone already half slipping from his fingers.

"My Tahoe?" His voice was low, dangerous, stripped of anything but raw intent.

"That's correct, sir. No driver. Doors open. Looks like it's been sitting maybe an hour. We're holding the perimeter until—"

The rest blurred in his ears. His chest burned with every breath. Kristen. Ellie. *No.*

Beside him, Casey swore under her breath and yanked her jacket off the chair. Her face went stone-hard, all trace of banter gone. "Then it's started."

Will was already moving, grabbing his coat with one hand, the other clenched so tight his knuckles went white.

His voice cut the air like a blade: "Call it in. Nobody touches that vehicle until we get there."

Casey fell into step, matching his pace as they pushed through the bullpen. "The ninth green, Will. That's not random. He's staging this."

Will didn't look at her, couldn't. His eyes were fixed forward, but his voice was hoarse with fury. "Then he's staging it for me."

The early-morning hum of the precinct faded behind them. Outside, the sky was just beginning to flash again with the kind of lightning that warns of an approaching storm, where the world feels hollow, expectant. Will shoved open the door to his unmarked SUV, hands trembling on the steering wheel as he turned the key.

Casey settled in beside him, checking her sidearm. "Deep breath, Anderson. If he wanted them dead, he wouldn't leave a breadcrumb like this. He wants you to see it."

Will's jaw flexed. His voice was almost a growl. "Then I'll see it. And when I do, I'll finish it."

The Tahoe's engine roared to life, headlights carving through the dark as they tore out of the lot toward the ninth green.

When All Is Lost

Will and Casey pulled up to the club grounds, headlights cutting across the damp grass. Even from a distance, the glare of floodlamps gave it away: a scene already alive with uniforms, radios hissing, yellow tape snapping in the breeze.

Kristen's SUV sat at an angle on the 9th fairway, driver's door wide open. Her purse was still in the seat, one heel abandoned in the grass a few feet away like she'd been yanked out mid-step, and an empty wine bottle beside the shoe.

Will's throat closed. He didn't even remember getting out of the car—just that his legs carried him forward before anyone could stop him.

"Sir—Detective—" a uniform started, but Casey waved him off. She stayed close at Will's shoulder, eyes sharp, jaw set.

The grass around the SUV bore deep impressions—drag marks toward the shadows, then nothing, tracks lost where the fairway met the rough.

"Where's the dash cam footage?" Will demanded, his voice too calm, too clipped.

"Already being pulled," the officer answered quickly. "But nothing live yet. No witnesses either. It's like the car just... appeared here."

Will leaned into the driver's side, eyes darting over every detail—the half-empty water bottle on the console, Kristen's phone still plugged into the charger, the driver's seat pushed back too far for her height. His pulse hammered in his ears.

"She didn't leave this here," he muttered. "She was forced."

Casey crouched by the shoe in the grass, studying the scuffed heel, the faint drag lines leading away. "He's staging this, Will. This isn't just abduction—it's theater. He wants us off balance."

Will straightened, chest burning, fists clenched at his sides. "Then where the hell is she now?"

The officer nearby shifted uneasily. "Detective, we're stretched thin. Everyone else is tied up on the wreck in the construction zone on the freeway. It's just us out here."

Will turned on him, voice sharp. "Then make the call anyway. We're going to need backup when he makes his next move."

Casey rose to her feet, gaze sweeping the wide, damp expanse of the fairway. The storm clouds still dragged low over the trees, the air heavy with static. "He hasn't finished setting the board," she said quietly. "This is just the opening shot."

Will looked back at the SUV, Kristen's purse sitting open on the seat like a taunt. His jaw tightened. "Then we find out what the next move is, before he makes it."

The Message

Emily lay on her bed, laptop still open, blue light humming against her skin. Her phone buzzed with a new notification.

Ellie: *Come to the course. Don't tell Mom or Dad.*

Emily frowned. *Seriously?* Ellie wasn't usually cryptic—annoying, sure, but not cagey.

Emily: *Are you kidding? I'll get in trouble with Mom if she finds out I snuck out again.*

Three dots pulsed. Then another message.

Ellie: *Mom won't mind. She's with me.*

Emily blinked, confused, a retort half-typed, when her phone buzzed again. This time it wasn't a text. It was a live video request.

She hesitated. Then tapped.

The screen filled with greenish light, turf lamps throwing jagged shadows across damp grass. A figure loomed near the lens, face hidden, voice electronically warped.

Behind him, bound and gagged, was Kristen. Her eyes were wide, pleading.

The camera tilted lower. Just long enough to catch a flash of color in the background. Bright shoes. Ellie's shoes were staged on top of some rolls of turf.

Emily's breath hitched, and her hand clapped over her mouth.

The video cut out. Her screen went black. Another text appeared.

Unknown: *Come alone to the course. Or the game ends.*

Emily sat frozen, phone clutched in white-knuckled hands. Her chest rose and fell in short, ragged bursts. She typed, deleted, typed again.

Emily: *This isn't funny. I'll tell Dad.*

The reply came instantly.

Unknown: *He can't save them. Only you can.*

Her phone trembled in her grip. Across the hall, her sister's door waited in the shadows, blank and impenetrable, as if daring her to open it.

She swallowed hard. Then stood.

Emily's breath caught in her throat. Her vision swam as she clutched the phone tighter, her pulse slamming in her ears. "Oh my God..."

The screen buzzed again. A final notification slid into view. This time, it wasn't a text; it was a three-second video.

She tapped.

A blur of her mother's face filled the frame, bound and terrified, lit by the harsh green glow of the course lights. The image vanished before Emily could even breathe.

Beneath it, a caption seared across the screen:
Your turn, twin.

Emily sat frozen, staring at the text long after the screen dimmed. The house was too quiet. Too still.

"Mom?" she called, voice small, hoping for an answer to end her nightmare. No reply. She crept down the hall, checking doors. Ellie's bed was empty, the covers a tangle. Kristen's room: the sheets were pulled back, her phone charger was empty, still hanging by the nightstand.

Emily's stomach bottomed out.

She ran downstairs, flicking on lights like it might conjure them out of the shadows. Nothing. The house was silent except for the hum of the refrigerator.

Dad. He still had to be here.

She tore through the kitchen, past the mudroom, into the garage. Will's SUV was gone. "He hadn't come home yet." Her knees buckled a little. He and Casey have been working late nights trying to catch these guys. If Dad hadn't been home, then he wouldn't have known.

Her throat closed. She grabbed her phone, thumb mashing Will's number. The call barely rang before she killed it, too jittery to wait for him to pick up. Tried again. Hung up again.

By the third attempt, she was sobbing in frustration as her car was already peeling out of the driveway, tires spitting gravel. "Why does this shit always happen to us!" She screamed, beating on the steering wheel.

"She thought about calling 911—but what would she even say? That a masked lunatic had sent her a text message from her sister's phone?"

Racing down the roadways, "Pick up, pick up, *please*—" She stabbed at Casey's contact. Once. Twice. Straight to voicemail. On the third try, the line clicked.

"Casey!" Emily practically screamed into the phone.

"Whoa—Emily? Slow down, what's—"

But she didn't slow down. The words spilled out rapidly: "Mom's gone, Ellie's gone, I got a text from Ellie's phone, but it wasn't her, it was him, and there was a video, golf course, and she was there, and he has her sneakers—"

Headlights sliced through the darkness like a blade, and the screech of brakes ripped across the quiet country club lot. Emily's car fishtailed slightly before jerking to a stop, her hands still white-knuckled on the wheel.

Will and Casey spun toward the noise, both halfway through the kind of clipped argument that came right before a move.

Emily pushed her door open, almost tripping as she hurried outside. Her face was streaked with tears, clutching her phone as if it were on fire. She staggered toward them, words spilling out in a frantic rush neither of them could understand yet.

Casey slowly lowered her phone from her ear, her eyes fixed on Emily's panic. For a moment, everything around them was quiet, every sound drowned out by what they were witnessing.

"Will," Casey said, her voice low and sharp, never taking her eyes off Emily. Then, with a dry bite that couldn't mask the dread in her tone, she said: "I've got a bad feeling about this."

Strike Plan

Emily practically crashed into Will's arms, her phone shoved at him with shaking hands. "Look!" she gasped. "Dad, look—"

On the screen: the hostage video. Grainy but clear enough, Kristen, bound and gagged, forced to her knees on the 18th green. Eldon Price stood over her, calm as a priest at mass. Floodlights blasted the turf around them, turning the scene into a sick stage.

In the corner, just barely visible behind stacked rolls of sod, were Ellie's sneakers. Bright blue, white Hoka lettering, unmistakable.

Will's stomach twisted, but his voice came out steady, low, his command tone. "Rivers needs to see this."

Minutes later, DHS's Evan Rivers pulled in with a full SUV from the field office in town. Doors swung open, tac gear unloading fast, boots hitting the grass. They huddled between the headlights, radios crackling, the night thick with tension.

"Damn," Casey muttered, watching them unload. "That's the fastest I've ever seen the government move." Her eyes swept the shadowed veranda, jaw tight. "We call for backup any other night, we're lucky if we get a voicemail."

She glanced toward the darkened clubhouse doors — too quiet, too still — and her mouth twisted into something caught between a grimace and a smirk. "Somebody tell Command to bring a Jedi," she said under her breath. "Because whoever's in there wiped this place cleaner than a mind trick."

Will didn't smile. "Let's hope they're still alive in there to save."

Rivers joined them at the line of SUVs, phone already to his ear. "Lucky for you, we were running night drills in the south lot. Pure coincidence — or maybe Price didn't check the calendar."

Will wasted no time. "Good. Get in touch with the mobile carrier; we'll need a live location on their cell phones. SouthernLink Wireless set it up for us once before. I want it now."

Rivers had a phone pressed tight to his ear, one finger jammed in the other to block out the hiss of radios and wind. He nodded sharply as he listened, then turned back to Will and Casey.

"They've already pulled the metadata," he said. "Order from last time was still active, so it cut through the red tape. SouthernLink pushed it live."

Another pause as he listened, jaw tightening. "Two hits. Area around the Eighteenth green—your wife's phone is pinging from the far side of the clubhouse. But there's a second signal fuzzy and may be underground, tracked to the old tunnel access beneath the course."

He lowered the phone, eyes hard. "He's splitting you."

Casey let out a sharp breath. "Then we split. No hesitation, no sitting around in the Jedi Council chamber debating. We move before this guy gets his Order 66 moment."

Will's head snapped toward her. "I'm going after Kristen."

"Fine," Casey shot back. "Then I'll take Ellie. She's been watching me, listening to me. If she's still alive, I can keep her focused, keep her from panicking. Call it... using the Force."

Will glared. "Casey, this isn't a movie."

"No kidding. Movies end after two hours," she said, eyes sharp. "This one's been playing for months."

Emily suddenly broke in, her voice cracking. "I'm coming. You can't leave me here while he—while they—"

"No," Will said, firm. "You stay here. No argument."

Emily's voice rose, desperate. "Dad, I can help!"

Casey crouched down in front of her, hands gripping her shoulders. Her tone softened, but the humor didn't quite leave. "Listen, kid. Every story needs somebody holding the line at home base. That's you. Leia didn't take down the Death Star by flying the X-wing herself; she trusted the people who could."

Emily blinked at her through tears. "This isn't a movie."

Casey smiled faintly. "Yeah, copycat, but sometimes the movies get it right." She squeezed Emily's shoulders tighter. "We'll bring them back. That's a promise."

Rivers chimed in, "Don't worry, Ellie, you are safe here with these officers, Finest Oakhaven PD has to spare at the moment." As the two officers guarding Kristen's SUV stepped toward Ellie.

Emily's lips trembled before she gave the slightest nod.

Casey straightened, her jaw set, already heading toward her team. "Alright then," she muttered, pulling her rifle River's had handed her into place. "Let's go rescue the princess."

Will scrubbed a hand down his face, muttering under his breath. "You really need new material."

Casey smirked over her shoulder. "Do not act like you are not Han Solo in this, Will. Grumpy, reluctant, but always saving the day. Me? I get the blaster and the bikini."

Will shook his head, but the corner of his mouth almost twitched upward before he forced it back down.

The teams split, North service stair to the irrigation tunnel; south line to the 18th tee boxes. Will and Rivers, with one of the Special Response Tac Team guys heading for Kristen on the 18th green, Casey and the remaining SRT team for the tunnels for Ellie. Emily stood under the glaring headlights, whispering like a prayer: *Bring them home.*

Shooting for Birdie

The 18th green had been transformed into a grotesque theater. Floodlights bathed the turf in a sterile glow, cutting stark shadows across the manicured grass. From a distance, it almost looked staged for a gala or a press conference —neat, symmetrical, deliberate —except for the scene at its center.

Eldon Price stood tall, framed by the light, his polo shirt crisp, his slacks pressed, his shoes polished to a shine. He could have been mistaken for one of the club's members posing for a brochure, a man who belonged here. But his eyes betrayed him. They burned with something wild, a fevered righteousness that twisted his every movement. His jaw worked tight, veins rising in his neck, fists clenched so hard around a 9-iron the knuckles had gone bone-white.

At his feet, Kristen knelt. Her wrists were lashed together in front of her, rope biting into raw skin. Her face was pale but her chin lifted, defiance radiating in the harsh light. Behind her, the flagpole rattled in the breeze, less a marker of the game than a banner planted in conquest.

The green was too perfect, too manicured, its very symmetry making her smallness feel deliberate, as if the space itself had been designed to showcase her vulnerability. Her knees dug into the wet turf, blades cutting through the thin fabric of her stockings. Every breath against the tape across her mouth came shallow, uneven, but her eyes never dropped.

It wasn't the pain hollowing her out. It was the silence.

The floodlights erased the horizon, turned the fairway into a blank stage where every shadow felt too deep, every brightness too cruel. Somewhere, she knew, cameras had to be rolling. That was his way. If her daughters were watching, if he meant this to be some twisted broadcast, then she would not break.

She had broken once before. She remembered that weight, that humiliation. She remembered swearing she would never let her daughters see her like that again.

So she lifted her chin higher. She met the night with steady eyes. If she had to bleed into this grass, she would do it staring Eldon Price in the face.

He seemed to sense her resolve. His hand clamped down on her shoulder, iron-strong, his breath hot at her ear. His whisper was thick with venom and scripture:

"Balance, Mrs. Anderson. Tonight the scales tip back where they belong."

Her pulse spiked, heat flooding her veins, but she didn't flinch. The tape muffled her breath, her chest rising fast, but she forced herself to stillness. She would not give him her fear.

And then, a sound. Subtle, almost lost beneath the wind rattling the flag.

A crunch. The weight of a bootstep pressing into wet turf, steady and deliberate.

Her heart leapt against the ropes, hope flaring bright and fierce. It was faint, but it was enough.

Her eyes burned as she drew one thought close, clutching it like a shield against the dark:

He's here. Will's here.

The footsteps drew closer in the darkness, slow and deliberate. Neither Kristen nor Price could tell who it was at first, just the steady crunch of boots through damp turf, cutting through the silence of the floodlit green.

Price's grip tightened on the 9-iron, his eyes flicking toward the shadows beyond the light. Kristen's chest constricted, heart hammering against the ropes.

Two figures ghosted along the edges, flanking wide, careful not to break the wash of the floodlights. Rivers and another SRT operator raised their rifles, staying just outside the beam.

Then, from the dark, Will stepped into the light.

Like a phantom pulled from the night itself, his gun was steady, his face carved into something unmovable. He wasn't just walking into a hostage scene; he was stepping into a sermon.

Price's voice rose, low and bitter, carrying across the manicured green like a curse. "They poisoned the soil, Detective. My family's land, erased from the maps. Their money bought silence, bought comfort, bought the illusion of untouchable lives. And what did we get?"

He spat onto the turf, the sound sharp in the quiet. "Cancer. Ruin. Graves."

His voice sharpened, teeth bared in a snarl, eyes blazing. "This—" His arm swept toward Kristen, toward the grotesque scene at his feet. "This is balance. This is justice. Returning the score to zero."

Will took another step forward, gun never wavering, every muscle taut. He'd seen zealots before, men who twisted their fury into holy math, convinced the scales of blood and fire answered only to them.

But he had never seen one standing over Kristen.

And that was a different kind of terror.

Beneath the club, the tunnels reeked of mildew and gasoline. The brickwork was slick with condensation; flashlight beams wobbled against curved walls that seemed to close in the deeper they went. Dust particles filled the beam, dancing, leading the way. Casey charged forward, side by side with one of the SRT guys, leading the way, her custom Sig Sauer 365XL Rose up, light braced in her other hand. Each step splashed through shallow puddles; it wasn't water, the echoes booming like cannon fire in the confined space.

Her gut twisted. The smell of gasoline, fuel oil, and diesel, along with bags of fertilizer, was deliberately stacked along the walls. This wasn't just a hiding place; it was a fuse waiting for a spark.

"Holy shit, it's a trap," her mind hissed.

She muttered under her breath, tightening her grip. "Great. Guess I get to go out like Alderaan. Big boom, no survivors."

The wide tunnel opened into a narrow chamber. Her boots crunched on broken gravel and glass as she stepped inside, the flashlight beam slicing through the dark.

Her beam swept the floor, slick with old water, glinting off rusted metal and streaks of something darker. The air was thick — mold, engine oil, blood, sweat — a smell that lived in the back of her throat like a threat. Concrete walls wept cold moisture in slow, steady drips. A chain hung slack from the ceiling, crusted with corrosion—a plastic tarp bunched in one corner, stained red-black.

The light caught movement.

Then landed on her.

Ellie.

Strapped to a metal chair bolted into the floor, zip ties biting into her wrists. Barefoot. A gag pulled tight across her mouth. Her dark hair was damp and matted to her forehead, a smear of blood across her temple. She flinched at the light — head jerking up, pupils blown wide.

For a heartbeat, she didn't seem to recognize Casey.

Then her eyes locked.

Panic flared — then something else: *relief*. Fragile. Raw.

Casey's breath caught in her throat. The sight of her — alive — broke something loose and brutal inside her. She moved fast, knees hitting concrete as she dropped beside her.

"Ellie. It's me. You're okay."

Ellie shook her head hard, chest heaving behind the gag.

Casey's hands moved quickly — scanning the restraints, checking for traps. The ties were layered, deliberate. Amateur, but cruel. Someone had taken their time.

She kept her voice low, steady. "I've got you. Don't move."

A single bulb overhead flickered once, casting long shadows along the walls. Every inch of Casey's skin prickled. She could feel it — they weren't alone in this place. Not really. Even if the captor was gone, his presence remained. The room still *hummed* with it.

A wire lay coiled behind the chair. Cables ran along the wall to a mounted camera — a lens. Live feed? Maybe.

She clicked off her flashlight. Drew her gun. Eyes scanning.

Then back to Ellie.

"I'm getting you out of here," she said, jaw tight.

Ellie's eyes brimmed, but she didn't cry. Not fully. Just one tear sliding down her cheek, silent.

Casey holstered her weapon and reached for her knife.

She pulled the gag free. Ellie coughed, voice shredded.

"I knew you'd come," she rasped.

"I've got you, kid!" Casey barked, moving fast. She kept her muzzle high while one of the SRT guys covered her flank. Casey had her ZT pocket knife already in her other hand; it opened with a flick of her index finger, and she slashed through the cords, nylon parting with sharp snaps. The blood-stained gag now hanging around her neck came last, flung aside into the dark.

Ellie coughed hard, gulping air, her whole body trembling. She tried to speak but broke into choked sobs.

"Save it," Casey told her, brisk but steady, hauling her up. "You don't need to talk. You need to move. We're not staying in this Death Star waiting for it to blow."

Ellie clung to her sleeve, grip iron-tight, no sarcasm, no defiance, just desperate relief.

The two SRT men exchanged a look before one spoke. "We'll sweep the rest of the line, check for victims. Tunnel bends west and connects near the clubhouse—we'll come out that way."

Casey nodded, though her eyes were fixed on the wall. Her flashlight beam caught a faint smear along the bricks – oily, dark, deliberate. It wasn't dirt. She'd noticed it on the way in but hadn't stopped. Now it made her stomach drop.

A burn line.

"Go," she said sharply, voice low. "Get anyone you find and move fast."

The SRT agents nodded, rifles angled low as they disappeared down the dark corridor.

Casey turned to Ellie. The girl's breathing was ragged, her hands shaking. "We're heading out," she said, forcing calm into her voice. "You see that light up ahead? That's your way out."

Ellie hesitated. "You're coming, right?"

Casey's light swept the wall again, catching the curve of wire coiled tight into the mortar. "In a minute," she said. "I need to check something."

"Casey—"

"Ellie." Her tone cuts through the panic, steady and unflinching. "You move now. Go outside; officers are waiting. You will see the lights. Run straight to them. Yell out so they can see you. Tell Will I'm right behind you."

Tears welled, but Ellie obeyed. She stumbled toward the faint light ahead, half-running, bare feet slapping against wet stone.

Casey crouched, tracing the wire with her gloved fingers. It ran straight into the tunnel wall — not deep, but enough to hide a trigger. Her throat went dry.

"Oh, motherfu-," she whispered, desperately reaching for her radio. "Command, we've got—"

The rest was swallowed by a thunderous *whump*.

The following explosion ripped through the passage like a living thing. A wave of heat punched her in the chest, light flared white, and then everything went silent.

Outside, Ellie burst from the tunnel mouth and fell hard into the grass. She turned back just in time to see the fire erupt — a roaring inferno that swallowed the tunnel entrance, then spat out debris, spraying across the fairway. The shockwave rolled over her, flattening her against the wet earth, singeing hair on her arms.

She screamed Casey's name, but the sound was lost beneath the blast.

For a few heartbeats, all she could hear was ringing — and then, faintly, the sound of falling ash.

The SRT agents were gone. The tunnel was gone. And Casey—

Ellie's sobs came out in ragged gasps. "She didn't make it... she didn't..."

No one was there to contradict her.

The firelight flickered across her face as she crumpled against the grass, clutching her knees, until at last she whispered, half to herself, "She said she'd be right behind me."

Back at the 18th green, the explosion thundered across the course, shook the ground so much the flag waved in the cup.

On the 18th green, Will flinched at the roar, the ground under his boots trembling. A column of fire clawed up from the far side of the clubhouse, curling into the night sky, lighting up the area.

Rivers' radio crackled with static, then went dead. His face tightened. "That was the tunnel that just went up! We're moving to assess."

Will's chest locked, eyes darting from the inferno back to Price standing in the floodlights. Kristen's wide eyes said what his gut already knew: Casey and Ellie had been down there.

For a split second, the green was a war zone waiting to erupt, fire behind them, zealot in front of them. And Will's world narrowed to one thought: *find them, now.*

Price's voice rose with fury, echoing across the manicured expanse like a sermon shouted from a pulpit. His words blurred into rage, but the intent was clear; his eyes were fixed on Kristen, who was bound hands and feet, mouth gagged, and helpless at his feet.

Price had raised and forced Kristen to her feet, pushing her in front of him like a shield. His voice rose in cadence now, each word sharpened with rage:

"They laughed at me, Detective!" Price's voice carried across the green, raw and sharp under the floodlights. "They drank their wine, they played their games, while the poison spread through our land. My sister—" his voice caught, rough with something that was almost grief, "— my sister Susan died coughing blood because of them. And not one of them paid."

Price recalled the smell of fertilizer and cut grass had once meant summer to Eldon Price. Back before the machines and the chemicals. Before his sister started coughing blood into a rag each morning.

He could still see his sister from her last year of life, thin as reeds, skin turned gray, eyes yellow at the edges. The doctor called it liver failure. Eldon knew better.

The creek behind their house had run brown for years now—tainted by runoff from the golf course and the factories the board had made quiet deals with. She used to play in that water, barefoot and laughing, sunlight catching in her hair. Back when it was clean. Back when Oakhaven still felt like home.

By the end, she couldn't even sip from a glass without retching.

The night she died, he walked the course alone. The fairways glistened under the floodlights, manicured and perfect, while she lay beneath uncut grass and cheap flowers. He stood in a bunker, toes sinking into the cool sand, and whispered his vow to the dark:

They poisoned you. They buried you. But I'll bury them too.

From then on, every rake, every divot, every blade of grass he touched wasn't just maintenance. It was preparation. The land itself would remember, and so would he.

Moonlight silvered the fairways now, sprinklers ticking in their patient rhythm.

Eldon Price walked the fifth hole alone, a rake balanced across his shoulder, boots pressing into the damp turf. The others had gone home hours ago. This was his time—the hour when the course grew quiet enough to listen.

He stopped at the edge of a bunker and let the rake slide down into the sand. His hand brushed the grains. This was the spot—the same one where he'd made his promise.

"They think the ground forgets," he murmured, his voice rasping. "But I don't. And neither do you."

The wind stirred through the pines, a faint hiss that sounded like agreement.

He straightened, surveying the fairway with a groundskeeper's eye. Every divot, every rake, every blade of grass—he knew them all by name. They weren't just tools anymore. They were instruments, waiting.

Eldon exhaled slowly, filling his lungs with the smell of wet earth and cut grass. Somewhere, men in suits still laughed and clinked their glasses, just as they had while his sister was dying.

But here, under the moon, the course belonged to him alone.

"Soon," he whispered, eyes on the flawless green. "Soon, they'll lie here too."

Present Time

Will's jaw flexed, his voice steady as stone. "No, Price. That wasn't justice. That was a tragedy. And now you're not honoring her—you're turning her grave into your excuse, disgracing her memory."

The words hit like a strike. For the briefest moment, Price froze, his breath catching, the iron shaft trembling in his grip. The conviction in his eyes wavered—just a flicker—before rage surged back, hotter, more unhinged.

"You think I don't know what she was?" he shouted. "She fought for people like your wife, the ones who argued for settlements, for quiet payouts. Lawyers who buried poison with paperwork." His lip curled. "Kristen Anderson — District Attorney. Defender of order, protector of the system. The very system that let my sister rot while it shook hands with murderers."

Kristen stiffened, her gag muffling the sound that tore up her throat. She shook her head violently, eyes wide, pleading, desperate to speak.

Price yanked her closer, using her like a shield, his voice dropping to a rasp. "You don't see it, Detective? She's their mouthpiece. Every board member, every contractor, every liar who called this progress — she made it legal. She gave them language for their sin."

Rain streaked his face, but the fury burning there wasn't wild anymore; it was cold, resolved. "So I chose her. Not because she signed the papers — but because she defended the people who did. Because her silence let it stand."

He jabbed the iron toward the ground again, voice rising into something that almost sounded like prayer. "She's the symbol. The clean hands of the guilty. When she falls, they all see their reflection."

Will took a step closer, slow and deliberate. The rain pattered against the brim of his jacket, faint and steady, like a metronome counting down to something inevitable.

"What about the cartel money, Price?" Will said, his voice low, measured. "The offshore accounts. The shell companies are tied to your name. Fake IDs found in your shed. That's not justice — that's criminal infrastructure. Who's bankrolling you?"

Price didn't move, but the tension in his jaw tightened.

Will's tone hardened. "You say you're cleansing the corruption, but what I see looks an awful lot like the same rot you claim to hate. The same networks. Same blood money. You attacking my partner — that wasn't some act of divine punishment. That was an ambush."

He took another step. "So tell me, Price — who are you working for? The board? The cartel? You pick a side, or are you freelancing as God's hitman tonight?"

The change was instant. Price's stillness shattered. His calm fury turned sharp, his voice cutting through the rain.

"You think I'd take their money?" he snarled, spitting the word like poison. "The same parasites who buy the silence of your bosses, who pour their blood cash into charity tournaments while the ground rots beneath our feet?"

He raised the broken nine-iron, the metal gleaming in the flash of lightning. "No. I used their greed. Their channels. I bled them dry the way they bled us. But I never served them. I never will."

Will didn't flinch. "Then explain the IDs. The transfers. The encrypted accounts in your name."

"I used them," Price snapped. "That's the language of the powerful, Detective. You want to fight corruption, you speak its tongue."

He jabbed the iron toward him, every word vibrating with conviction. "But don't you dare put me in their pocket. Don't you dare. I don't know anything about your partner — never met him."

Will's eyes narrowed. "'Him?'"

Price blinked, thrown for just a second.

"My partner," Will said evenly, "is a woman. Detective Casey Murphy. She's the one you tried to kill in that tunnel."

For a moment, confusion flickered in Price's eyes — then twisted into contempt. "A woman?" he said, the word curling out like a sneer. "You sent a woman into that hole? Into *my* ground?" He shook his head, a bitter laugh scraping through his throat. "That tunnel was a grave waiting to happen, Anderson. It would've swallowed anyone who stepped inside, anyone who was already inside. I didn't set the blast — your people did that years ago when they let greed rot the foundations."

He took a step closer, his voice dropping to a hiss. "But maybe that's the problem, isn't it? You keep putting women in men's wars, expecting them to walk out. The world's not built for that kind of mercy."

Kristen flinched at the venom in his tone, the way he said *women* like it was a weakness carved into bone.

Will's jaw tightened. "You sound a lot like the men you claim to hate."

Price's eyes burned in the half-light, his grip on the iron whitening. "Don't twist this. I didn't kill her. The tunnel was judgment — not by my hand, but by the earth itself. The same earth those bastards poisoned. It took her the same way it took my sister."

He jabbed the iron toward the ground, voice rising. "You call that murder? I call it the land remembering."

240

Will's stomach twisted. "The tunnel," he said slowly, realization cutting through the rain. "You set the charges. You tied Ellie there."

Price's smile was faint, chilling in its calm. "A lure, Detective. Nothing more. The innocent must sometimes be used to draw out the guilty. She was never meant to burn. Only to bring your partner running. But the earth decided differently."

Kristen's strangled scream tore through the gag—raw, animal, breaking on the edge of breath. Her knees buckled, wrists twisting against the ties until her skin split. The sound shredded through Will. He'd heard death in every form—gunfire, silence, last words whispered into the dark—but never this. Never a mother hearing that her child was gone by the man responsible —not only that, but his child.

He couldn't breathe. Couldn't think. Images slammed through him in flashes: Ellie's laughter spilling through the kitchen, her sneakers by the back door, the last text she'd sent—*Love you, old man.* Casey's voice right after that, steady, confident: *I'll bring her home.*

And now both are gone.

Will's finger brushed the trigger, his pulse roaring in his ears. Every inch of him screamed to pull it, to end this, to tear through the distance between them and wipe that sick, righteous calm off Price's face, forever.

But Price only smiled, bitter and broken. "You see?" he whispered. "Even now, you protect her. You protect *them.* The guilty. The ones who built all this rot."

Will steadied his aim, his voice a low rasp. "And what does that make you, Eldon? A gardener with blood on his hands?"

The iron shook once in Price's grip, his breath heaving, rain dripping from his brow like sweat. "No," he said, almost reverent. "It makes me the one man who finally stopped waiting for rain to wash the filth away."

Will could barely hear him anymore. Kristen was shaking violently now, sobbing into the gag, her eyes pleading with him—not to shoot, not to make her watch another person die, not when they'd already lost everything.

Instead, Price straightened, chest heaving. "This isn't their game, Detective. This is mine. I set the course. I keep the score. And tonight—" his gaze cut down at Kristen, "her round ends. Now!"

Price's eyes glistened in the light. For a heartbeat, Will thought he saw hesitation.

And then—

"Hey, asshole!"

The shout cracked across the green like a gunshot, slicing through the rain and smoke.

Price's head snapped toward the sound.

From the shadows at the edge of the floodlights, Casey emerged — limping, soaked, her face streaked with soot and blood. The right sleeve of her jacket hung in tatters, scorched at the edge, and a thin line of crimson ran from her temple down to her jaw. Her eyes, though — sharp, green, alive — burned hotter than the tunnel fire she'd just crawled out of.

Steam curled off her clothes, the lingering ghost of the blast still clinging to her. She looked like she'd been swallowed by the earth and clawed her way back out.

Behind her, Ellie stumbled forward, clutching her arm to her chest, her face pale and tear-streaked but alive. Her breathing was ragged, but her gaze locked on her mother the instant she saw her — that slight, broken sound she made hitting Will harder than the explosion ever could.

Kristen's muffled sob tore through the gag, her whole body collapsing with relief even as she trembled uncontrollably.

Will's heart slammed against his ribs — a rush of disbelief and savage relief colliding all at once.

Casey — bloodied, unbreakable.

Ellie — alive.

The nightmare cracked open just enough to let light in.

Price froze. His grip faltered for the first time, eyes darting between them like a cornered animal seeing ghosts crawl out of the grave.

Then the snarl came — low, guttural, animal. Rage tore across his face, burning away the shock.

He jerked on Kristen's restraints, whipping her around, then shoved Kristen to her knees, the gag ripping from her mouth as Price used it to steady her head. The broken 9-iron came up over his head, gleaming under the floodlights like a blade of judgment.

Will shifted his aim, finger tightening — but Kristen was still too close, half-collapsed in the arc of his strike. The shot wasn't clean. One wrong pull, and he'd take her with the monster.

For a heartbeat, everything froze — rain hanging in the air, breath locked in every throat.

Then the night exploded.

A flash.

A thunderclap.

The world kicked back from the sound.

Price jerked — once, hard — the 9-iron slipping from his hand as if cut loose by the blast itself. He staggered two steps, eyes wide with shock, before collapsing to his knees. The weapon hit the grass beside Kristen with a dull, wet thud.

Smoke curled through the mist. The echo of the gunshot rolled off into the trees.

Will blinked, his ears ringing and vision narrowing, as everything suddenly moved again—Kristen crying, face pressed against the ground, Price toppled forward, and the lingering scent of cordite smoldered in the darkness surrounding them.

Price lay dead, blood spreading across the manicured perfection he had claimed as his altar.

Kristen sobbed, tried to get up, half-collapsed, until Will caught her in his arms, immediately started ripping and cutting her bonds free.

Casey lowered her weapon, chest heaving, eyes blazing like she'd just fired the last shot in a galactic war. "Yeah," she muttered under her breath. "Leia shoots first."

Ellie, who had been frozen in time, just beyond the fringe of the green, broke toward Casey, stumbling across the green until she caught up to Casey.

And for the first time in hours, Will let himself believe, however briefly, that they had won.

"I thought y'all were gonna leave me down there," Ellie whispered, voice thin and raw.

Casey forced a crooked grin, brushing a strand of sweaty hair back from the girl's face. "Kid, I don't do carbonite."

Ellie gave a weak laugh that broke into a sob, burying her face against Casey's shoulder.

The green was chaos then, Rivers and tac moving in, securing the body, lights glaring, radios crackling. But for Will, for Kristen, for Casey, and Ellie, it all blurred into background noise.

When Will finally realized that Kristen and Ellie had found safety, Will stumbled backward and collapsed onto the grass, the adrenaline drain leaving him empty. He pressed his palms to the turf, breathing heavily, eyes fixed on the night sky.

Casey walked over, boots dragging through the wet grass, her silhouette still haloed in the smoke drifting across the green. The blast had left its mark — her jacket torn, soot streaked up her neck, a thin cut running from her temple to her jaw. Her hair hung loose and damp, strands plastered to her face, but her eyes — sharp and green — still burned bright.

She dropped beside Will, sitting cross-legged before flopping back with a groan, staring up at the floodlights that painted the night sky a harsh, artificial white. For a long moment, neither spoke. Just the sound of distant sirens and the hum of the lights above them.

Will groaned, rubbing his eyes with the heel of his hand. "I'm too old for this shit."

Casey tilted her head toward him, a crooked grin ghosting through the grime and blood. "Yeah, well... at least you didn't get frozen in carbonite."

That cracked him up. His laugh came out rough — half a choke, half disbelief — but real. He shook his head, smiling despite himself.

Casey sat up again, surveying the scene—blood staining the hole, ropes where Kristen had been tied. Her voice softened, almost reverent: "We finished this one."

Will propped himself on an elbow, watching Kristen with Ellie. His reply was quiet but steady: "No. We just moved to the next hole."

Silence pressed in, broken only by the hum of radios and the low murmur of DHS agents locking down the green. Sheriff's deputies trickled in next, delayed by the interstate gridlock. That was Oakhaven's curse; hemmed in by the lake, there was no shortcut. You couldn't drive through water.

For the first time in hours, neither detective moved.

Finally, Casey nudged his shoulder. "So, Detective... you buying the first round after this?"

Will's mouth tugged into a tired half-smile. "Only if you bring the cigars."

He pushed himself to his feet, knees protesting, and offered her a hand up. "I'll bring the bourbon. Back patio. Anderson house."

Casey took his hand, her grip firm despite the faint tremor in her arm. "Deal," she said, breath hitching into something almost like a laugh. "Make it Eagle Rare—I'm gonna need top-shelf anesthesia for this headache."

He chuckled, low and ragged, as he helped her to her feet. Together they stood in the silver wash of the floodlights, the green still scarred with shadows and fog.

For a long moment, neither spoke. The echoes of gunfire lingered somewhere between their ribs—heavy, remembered.

Not victory.

Not closure.

Just survival.

For now.

Aftermath on the Green

The medics arrived, once they were notified, the scene was clear, and they moved fast, swarming Kristen first. They shone lights into her eyes, checked her pulse, and examined the raw rope burns that circled her wrists. She barely registered them. Her grip was locked on Will's jacket, knuckles white.

"I thought it was the end," she whispered hoarsely, fragments spilling as though she couldn't stop them. "I thought he'd—" Her words broke into sobs, jagged and unstoppable. She pressed her face against Will's chest, shuddering.

Will closed his eyes and let out a breath he hadn't realized he'd been holding since the SUV was found on the fairway. His arms wrapped around her, protective, immovable. His hand rested against the back of her head, and he pressed his cheek to her hair. His jaw tightened hard enough to ache, as if clamping down on everything he couldn't afford to say. Relief. Rage. The near-loss of her replaying in an endless loop.

A shout cut through the static of radios and medic calls.

Emily.

She was sprinting down the slope of the 18th green, her sneakers slipping in the damp grass. Rivers tried to intercept her, but she ducked under his arm and ran straight for Ellie.

Ellie staggered forward, rope marks still visible around her ankles, and nearly threw herself into her twin's arms. The collision almost knocked them both over, their grip on each other frantic and desperate. Ellie's body shook as she buried her face against Emily's shoulder.

"I thought I could outsmart him," Ellie gasped, voice breaking into hiccups. "I thought if I played along, we'd catch him—"

Emily clutched her tighter, her own words tumbling out in a rush. "I followed Mom out the door to check on the car windows left down. I just went to check my car. He was waiting. He tied me up and made Mom drag me down there, Ellie, hands behind my back, tape on my mouth. I couldn't breathe; I couldn't move. And then he—" Her voice cracked, but she forced it out. "He took my shoes. Said I didn't deserve to wear them. And then he dragged Mom away. I thought he was going to kill us."

Ellie pulled back just enough to stare at her, tears burning hot down her cheeks. "God, Em... I should've listened to you. You told me I was reckless. You told me I wasn't untouchable." She shook her head, pressing her forehead against her sister's. "You were right. I should've listened all along."

Emily's fingers dug into her sister's sleeves, fierce despite the trembling in her hands. "We're both idiots. But we're still here. We are all still here. He was disqualified from his game. He can't mess with you anymore."

Ellie let out a wet laugh, almost a sob, and hugged her again, harder, so hard that a medic finally backed away, recognizing the moment was untouchable.

A few yards off, Casey stood with her arms crossed, her Sig finally holstered. Her posture was guarded, but her face betrayed her—soft, fierce, protective. For all her sarcasm and sharp edges, she looked like she'd take on an army if anyone so much as looked at those girls again.

Will glanced up, met her eyes across the chaos. He gave her one slow, deliberate nod. Gratitude. Respect. Trust.

Casey's chin dipped once in return, her mouth twitching with something caught between pride and exhaustion.

An EMT walked up and guided her toward the back of a waiting ambulance, a bloodied bandage pressed to her temple. She resisted at first—typical Casey—but the medic was firm, and Will could see the faint tremor in her legs. He followed a few steps, staying close, his presence grounding more than guarding.

"Just a concussion check," the medic said, running a light across her eyes. "You're lucky you didn't catch the brunt of that blast."

"Luck," Casey muttered, wincing as the light hit her pupils. "Sure. Let's call it that."

She caught Will's look and gave a faint smirk. "We stopped Price tonight... but McBride's killer? That one's still out there."

The words lingered in the air, heavy, unshakable. Will's jaw clenched as he gave a grim nod, the truth settling over them like fresh weight pressing against old scars.

Then it came—faint, drifting, impossible. That perfume. The same one. Slipping through the night air like a memory that refused to die. Here. Again.

Rivers caught up to them near the cruisers, his face drawn tight under the strobing lights. "One more thing you need to know. Financial Crimes pulled records this morning. It wasn't Price. Gregory Young was moving money under his name. All of it. Price never touched cartel cash."

Casey let out a sharp, disbelieving breath. "So Price was just a cover."

Rivers nodded once. "Young's the one you want."

Will's jaw hardened, but his voice stayed even. "Then Price was telling the truth. It was Young. That's where we look next."

Rivers moved off toward the command vehicles, barking into his radio. Casey sat on the edge of the ambulance bumper, a medic still cleaning the gash along her hairline. The floodlights painted everything sterile and white, too bright for a night that had already burned so much.

"Yeah," she murmured to herself, almost too quiet for the others to hear. "I told you I don't do carbonite."

A few techs nearby chuckled without context, but Will caught it. He shook his head faintly, the corner of his mouth tugging despite the tension, then turned back toward Kristen—his expression hardening again as the weight of what was next settled over them both.

Behind them, the fairway was littered with the remnants of Price's final stand—discarded zip ties, the 9-iron abandoned on the grass, tactical boot prints pressed deep into the turf. Floodlights still blazed, throwing long shadows across the green.

But for the first time that night, the scene no longer felt like a battlefield.

It felt like survival.

From the tree line beyond the rough, a faint click whispered in the dark. The lens of a camera glinted once in the floodlights' halo.

One of the uniforms swept a flashlight across the shadows, just for a second. The beam caught on something—bright blue sneakers, a flash so fast it could've been a trick of the eye. Then it was gone, swallowed back into the dark.

Price was finished.

But McBride's killer?

Still watching.

Still waiting.

The Roll Call

Three days later, Oakhaven's town square stood hushed beneath the weight of loss. The town wanted to have a separate memorial for the fallen heroes. Federal flags hung low beside the county's, their colors muted in the gray morning light. At the front, two portraits rested on easels draped in black cloth: Special Agents Nick Carter and John Ruiz, the DHS–SRT operators who hadn't made it out of the tunnels.

Captain Monroe read their names aloud, his voice measured but heavy. He spoke of sacrifice, of men who ran toward danger so others could walk away. Agent Rivers stood to the side in full dress, jaw locked tight, his silence saying more than words could.

Then came the roll call. The dispatcher's voice carried across the crowd:

"Special Agent Carter?"

Silence.

"Special Agent Ruiz?"

Silence.

Each name called twice more, each unanswered echo settling into the bones of everyone listening.

Kristen stood with Emily and Ellie just behind the first row. Emily wore her hair loose and plain black over her shoulders. But Ellie, she had chosen carefully. A black blouse tucked into a black skirt, cinched at the waist with a bold royal blue band. A quiet echo of the Thin Blue Line flag. Not loud, not ostentatious, but a statement that anyone in uniform recognized the moment their eyes landed on her.

The small handbag she carried looked almost out of place in her grip, but she clutched it tightly as the names were read, as the rifles cracked their salute outside, as the bugler's notes bent and broke in the humid night.

While gathering, more than one deputy brushed her shoulder in passing, no words, just the faintest nod. Ellie lowered her eyes but held herself straighter, as if the blue at her waist wasn't just fabric but a thread binding her to something larger than herself.

Ellie squeezed Emily's hand, whispering just loud enough for her family to hear: "They saved me. They saved us."

Casey shifted beside Will, the black band of her jacket crisp against the gray sky. A faint bruise still shadowed her temple beneath a small strip of medical tape, the only visible reminder of the blast. Her usual edge was muted; no smirk, no easy sarcasm to fill the silence. She just stood with her chin high, eyes bright but tired, the wind tugging at the loose strands of her red hair.

When the rifles fired their salute and the bell tolled, Will finally spoke, low enough that only she caught it:

"Everyone matters. Even when the board doesn't see them."

Casey's throat worked as she swallowed hard. Her reply came softer than her usual bite:

"And when they fall, the rest of us don't forget."

When the families stepped forward with roses, Ellie broke from her mother's side. Her voice trembled but carried through the hush: "I'm grateful. For what they did. For saving me. For saving us." She laid her rose against the portrait, her chin lifting despite the tears in her eyes.

The bugle's last note drifted on the air, haunting and unshakable.

When the crowd finally broke, people moved in hushed tones, but the weight stayed behind, stitched into Oakhaven for good.

When the crowd thinned, Captain Monroe found Will at the edge of the scene, away from the cluster of uniforms. His hat was tucked under his arm, his voice rougher than usual.

"You did good work this week, Anderson. Both of you did." His gaze flicked briefly toward Casey, then back. "We'll never square the ledger for those two agents... but you made sure there weren't more names on that list."

Will didn't answer at first. His jaw tightened, eyes scanning the chairs where the portraits were still displayed. "Doesn't feel like enough."

Monroe let out a long breath, the kind that seemed to carry years with it. "It never does. That's the curse of this job: we only remember the names we lose. Not the ones we save." He clapped a hand on Will's shoulder, firm. "Go home. Be with your family. That's how you honor them."

For once, Will didn't argue.

Monroe gave a final nod to Will and then to Casey, then stepped back toward a crowd of deputies, his silhouette folding into the haze of uniforms, sunlight, and the trees' shadows.

Casey hung back near the side of the building, jacket off, sleeves rolled, staring at the flag at half-mast. Her cigar box sat unopened in her hands, suddenly feeling like a weight she couldn't justify lighting.

Rivers found her there. His suit didn't quite hide the soldier, close-cropped hair, the rigid set of his shoulders. He had ditched the earpiece and the formality, just another man trying to stand still after too much motion.

"They were mine," he said, voice low, not looking at her yet. "My responsibility."

Casey shook her head, jaw tightening. "They were with me in that tunnel. They told me to run the kid out, and I did. I left them there. That's what I carry."

Rivers finally turned, eyes sharp but not unkind. "No. They made the call. They knew exactly what it meant. That's what operators do: buy time, buy ground, whatever it takes to get civilians out. And you brought Ellie back breathing. That's the win they wanted."

Her mouth twisted into a grimace mixed with a half-formed curse. "Some win. I keep seeing their faces, replaying when I turned around, aware that their exit behind me was in flames. It's as if I took the air from their lungs."

For a beat, Rivers didn't answer. Then he set his hand on her shoulder, firm. "Murphy, you didn't steal a damn thing. You honored their choice. You think they'd rather the story end with you and that kid buried down there too? You were their mission."

Casey's throat worked. She nodded once, sharply, and swiped at her face with the heel of her hand like she was chasing off sweat. "Doesn't make it any lighter."

"Never does," Rivers admitted. His voice dropped, raw for once. "But their families know they didn't die for nothing. That's because of you. Carry it, but carry it as theirs, not yours alone."

Finally, she met his eyes. "Guess we both lost people that night."

"Yeah," Rivers said, stepping back, straightening like he was putting his armor back on. "But we didn't lose the Andersons. And I'll take that trade, every time."

He drew himself upright, the vulnerable edge gone, mask of control locked firmly in place again: Ellie, standing small and solemn, dressed in a black blouse and skirt cinched at the waist with royal blue, a tiny handbag clutched tight at her side. She had clearly been there long enough to hear.

Rivers' face softened, just for a beat. Then he gave Casey the faintest nod and walked away, leaving the space for her.

Casey turned and froze when she saw Ellie. The girl's eyes were wide, rimmed red. Her voice cracked: "They... they died because of me."

Casey shook her head hard, stepping closer. "No, kid. Don't even start with that. They died because they chose to. Their choice. To protect you. You honor them by living. Not by drowning in guilt."

Ellie's lip trembled. "I don't know if I can."

Casey softened, voice firm but gentle, steel wrapped in cloth. "Then I'll teach you. One day at a time. You keep breathing, keep moving, keep fighting. That's how you carry them. Remember."

Ellie hugged her small handbag tighter, as if it were a shield. Casey popped open the cigar box, pulled one smooth stick, and tucked it neatly inside the bag.

"Don't ever light it," Casey told her. "Just keep it. A reminder that you walked out when you weren't supposed to. That's your marker. Their marker."

Ellie looked down at the bag, then back at Casey, tears cutting tracks down her cheeks. Her whisper was shaky but confident: "I'll carry it."

Casey gave a sharp nod, fierce and proud. "Damn right you will."

Ellie stepped forward and wrapped her arms around her. It wasn't a gentle hug—it was desperate, clinging, as if Casey were the last steady thing left standing in the world.

Epilogue: Two on the Board

Inside the Anderson House

That night, the Anderson house glowed like a lantern against the dark. Inside, the quiet wasn't heavy like it had been on the green; it was gentler, softer, the kind of quiet that comes when you've survived something, and the walls themselves seem to hold you steady.

The twins curled under their blanket on the couch, half-bickering over what to stream, half-dozing against each other. Kristen lingered in the doorway, phone to her ear, her voice a little too steady when Billy called to check in.

"Billy?" Her voice was steady, but tighter than she meant it to be.

On the other end, the hum of campus life bled through: voices, laughter, someone calling out across a quad. "Yeah, Mom. I just heard. Chapel Hill Police said an incident occurred at the club, and I need to call you guys. Said Captain Monroe contacted them and had them do a welfare check on me. It's all over text chains. Are you guys okay?"

Kristen forced a smile he couldn't see. "Well, your dad was trying to call, and things were a little hectic. The captain offered to run you down with his contacts up there in North Carolina. We're fine. Everyone's safe. Your sisters are right here."

Emily leaned closer, making sure her voice carried. "We're okay, Billy."

Ellie swiped the phone before she could answer. "Don't go all protective big-brother mode. We've got like three bodyguards now. You worry about not failing calc."

"Or getting your ass kicked on the lacrosse field," Emily chimed in, smirking.

Kristen plucked the phone back, sighing softly. "We'll keep you updated. You focus on school. No driving home tonight. We've got this covered. Love you."

Billy hesitated. "Love you guys. Call me if... anything changes."

When the line went dead, Kristen stayed still, staring at her daughters huddled under their blankets. For a moment, her smile slipped, and her free hand trembled against her side. She shoved the phone into her pocket, pulled a steady breath, and turned away before they could see.

On the Patio

Out back, the night was heavy but quieter, the hum of cicadas carrying under the porch light.

Casey and Will sitting and unwinding in their usual fashion.

Will leaned into his chair, glass in hand, his voice low. "Price didn't kill McBride. Which means someone else out there still has a scorecard."

Casey exhaled, watching the smoke curl off the cigar tip she'd lit. "Yeah. And whoever it is? They're not playing the same game Price was. Different target, different motive."

Will's jaw tightened. "Question is... who, and why?"

Casey shrugged, though her eyes stayed sharp. "Guess we'll find out when they want us to. Just hope it's not tonight. I need a break from all the insanity."

She cracked open her cedar box and plucked out another stick. A half-burned Acid Blondie balanced between her fingers, honey-sweet smoke curling into the dark. She slid one across the table toward him.

"Go on, Anderson. Live a little. Pairs better with that bourbon than you think."

Will shot her a flat look. "I don't smoke."

Casey smirked. "You don't *yet*."

"Didn't stop you from lecturing me last time," she said. "You don't smoke yet, we will see." She clipped the tip for him anyway, holding it out like a dare. "Smooth, sweet, won't kill you in one puff. Think of it as a tactical palate cleanser."

He hesitated, then accepted. The first drag made him cough hard enough that Casey grinned.

"Easy, cowboy. Sip it, don't wrestle it."

Will tried again, slower. The flavor surprised him, earthy, edged with vanilla, blending with the *Buffalo Trace* bourbon in a way that almost worked. He exhaled a thin ribbon of smoke and shook his head. "Not bad."

Casey leaned back, satisfied, her grin curling. "Told you. Sweet burn. Keeps the demons off the green."

Will tipped his glass toward her. "Or maybe it just makes you louder."

Will's gaze drifted from the bourbon glass to the angry red line along Casey's temple, a crescent where the med-tape had been. The porch light caught it just right, turning it into a shadow before the dark took it back.

He nodded toward it. "You never did tell me how you got out."

Casey's lips twitched, not quite a smile. "Out of the tunnel?"

Will gave a quiet grunt.

She leaned back, eyes fixed on the black stretch of trees beyond the yard. "I was halfway down the access run when it went up. One second, it was quiet—the next, the world turned inside out. Fire sucked the air out of the tunnel before I could even breathe. I went from standing, tracing the line, to feeling the shockwave before I heard it."

Her voice dropped. "Everything went orange. I thought... that was it. I don't even remember hitting the wall. When I came to, I was face-down in dust and debris, and I couldn't hear a damn thing. Just heat and ringing, head throbbing. The air was so thick, I couldn't tell which way was up."

She rubbed the side of her neck as if still remembering. "There was this drainage break—a split in the tunnel line where the runoff pipes cut through. I crawled until the smoke thinned and daylight began to leak in. That's when I saw her."

Will's grip on his glass tightened, knuckles pale.

Casey's eyes softened, the memory catching in the reflection of the porch light.

"Ellie was on her knees in the grass, right outside the opening," she said quietly. "She thought I was dead. She was shaking so hard she could barely hold herself upright—mud, soot, tears... she was rocking, like her body was trying to keep breathing even after her mind gave up."

Her voice thinned. "I called her name once. Nothing. Twice. Then she turned."

Casey swallowed hard, staring past the porch rail as if she could still see it. "That look on her face, Will—she didn't believe I was real. She just stared, like she was afraid that if she blinked, I'd vanish."

She gave a small, unsteady laugh. "Then she ran. Knocked me flat on my ass, right back into the grass. Neither of us could stop shaking. Didn't matter. She just kept saying it—'You're real. You're real.' Like if she stopped, I'd disappear again."

The porch fell silent except for the faint buzz of the night.

"Luck," Will said finally. His voice was low, rough.

Casey's eyes found his again, tired but sure. "Yeah," she said. "Luck. And one hell of a brave kid."

Will raised his glass. "To brave kids."

Casey clinked hers against his, the sound soft but steady. "And the stubborn idiots who run into tunnels after them."

The laughter from inside drifted through the open door—a fragile, living sound—and for the first time in a long while, it didn't feel haunted.

The Sermon Video

Then Will's phone buzzed on the table. The screen lit with a notification: **New Sermon Video.**

The air changed.

He opened it, handheld footage, shaky, weaving through the crowd at a weekend street market. Stalls lined the walkway, voices blurred in the background. And then, Emily and Ellie.

The camera trailed them too closely, lingering as Ellie brushed her hair back, and Emily paused at a honey vendor. The lens tilted down to catch the Oakhaven Knights logo on her chest, panning down to their legs, their shoes, and back up again. Neither looked up. Neither noticed.

Will's chest locked. The timestamp in the corner indicated that it was **that afternoon.**

The distorted voice whispered, intimate, as if pressed to his ear:

"Two pawns side by side.
Exposed. Ripe for the file.
Two on the green... perfect aim.
The Rook cannot guard both of them.
And I never miss my move."

Will's blood went cold.

The video ended, leaving only their reflections in the black glass of Will's phone — his face and Casey's, warped beside the frozen image of his daughters laughing.

For a long beat, the only sounds were the cicadas outside and the twins' muffled laughter drifting through the walls.

Will's jaw flexed, his pulse steady but hard. "They're just kids," he said quietly. "And somehow, they're still paying for our ghosts."

Casey leaned back in her chair, eyes fixed on the still frame of the girls at the market. She exhaled a stream of smoke, the curl rising between them like a flare against the dark.

"Then we don't give him a chance to touch them," she said, voice low and steady. "He wants a hunt? Fine. But I'm done pretending to be the Jedi in this story." Her eyes flicked to Will, cold and unblinking. "This time, I burn the Empire to the ground."

Will studied her in the dim porch light — not the badge, not the uniform, but the woman beneath it. The one who'd dragged herself out of fire and smoke to save his daughter.

He saw it now, clear as the scar at her temple: this wasn't bravado. It was exhaustion hardened into resolve. A lifetime of carrying ghosts had stripped away everything but purpose. She'd lost too many, buried too many, and something in her had finally decided—no more.

Her shoulders were squared, but not proud; it was the posture of someone bracing for the next hit and daring it to land.

Will's throat tightened. He'd watched trauma grind men down before, turn them brittle or cruel. But with Casey, it had done something different. It had reforged her. And tonight, staring at that frozen image of his girls on the phone screen, he understood—she wasn't just his partner anymore. She was family.

She was protecting what was left of theirs.

He exhaled, slow and steady, setting the glass aside. "You've had enough," he said quietly. Not a question. A truth.

Casey didn't look at him. Her jaw flexed once. "Yeah," she murmured. "And I'm not letting them take what's ours."

Will nodded, a grim weight behind it. "Then we burn the Empire together."

The words hung between them, heavy but shared, a vow whispered in bourbon and smoke.

From inside came the sound of Ellie's laughter — bright, fragile, unknowing — the kind of sound that made people like them keep fighting.

Will glanced toward the window, then back to Casey. "They're our reason," he said.

Casey's eyes flicked toward the glass, softer now. "And our line in the sand."

Outside, the cicadas droned, the night deepened — and somewhere out there, the Watcher kept moving.

But for now, on that porch, the war had already begun.

Casey left not long after midnight. The fence gate creaked once, then eased shut behind her, leaving only the echo of her boots on the gravel drive. Will sat there for a while, listening until the sound faded into the hum of cicadas and the low rustle of trees.

The porch felt emptier without her — not because of silence, but because she'd taken something with her when she left. Resolve. Defiance. Whatever you wanted to call it, it was the thing that kept them both moving forward when everything else fell apart.

He stared at the glass still sitting beside her chair. Half a finger of bourbon caught the porch light, trembling faintly with each breath of wind. The faint curl of smoke from her last bit of cigar still hung in the air, dissolving slow and stubborn.

Will rubbed a hand over his face, the weight of it all pressing down again. He'd seen what trauma did to people — how it didn't just scar, it rewired. Casey had spent years holding other people's lives together while her own kept splintering underneath. And tonight, when she'd made that promise — *no mercy, no rules* — he knew she'd meant it.

She'd crossed that invisible line where justice becomes personal, where survival starts to sound like vengeance.

He didn't blame her. Not for a second.

But he also knew what it would cost.

Will looked through the window into the living room. The girls were asleep now, tangled in a shared blanket, the soft rhythm of their breathing just visible in the rise and fall of fabric. Innocent, for now. Unaware.

His hand tightened on the back of the empty chair beside him — hers.

"She's protecting you," he murmured quietly, voice almost swallowed by the night. "Even if it kills her."

The words hung there, fragile and final.

Out in the yard, the motion light blinked on, catching the trees in a wash of pale gold before going dark again.

Will didn't move. He just stood there, watching the shadows shift across the lawn, thinking of Casey out there somewhere — still moving, still burning, still ready to go to war for his family.

And for the first time in a long while, he wasn't sure who he was more afraid for — her, or the man who came after them next.

Watcher's Journal:

He has been warned, but will he make a move?

Two pawns on the same file.
Sisters, side by side.
One shields, one sacrifices.
They think the King will save them.
But I've already mapped their lines.
The Rook cannot move backward.

The watcher set down the pawn in hand and closed their journal. The next move was already written.

Author Bio

Mark Harrington is a crime novelist and former law enforcement professional with more than twenty years of experience across North and South Carolina. He's investigated the kinds of cases—and met the kinds of people—that linger long after the files are closed.

A lifelong student of the *whodunit* genre, Harrington grounds his fiction in real crimes, firsthand witness accounts, and the late-night conversations officers share when the shift runs long and the coffee runs strong.

His stories are driven by character—real people, not perfect ones—each reflecting pieces of the flaws, fears, and courage found in all of us.

Harrington's influences range from the atmospheric grit of Raymond Chandler to the pulse-pounding thrillers of James Patterson, John Grisham, Michael Connelly, Jack Carr, Tom Clancy, and Stephen Hunter.

His debut novel, *Demon of Oakhaven*, introduced Detectives Will Anderson and Casey Murphy. His latest book continues their story, raising the stakes and revealing new fault lines in the city they serve.

He lives in South Carolina with his close-knit family of five—each with an "M" name—who like to joke that when he's at his desk, he's not plotting murders, just plotting the next twist.

Also by W Mark Harrington
Demon of Oakhaven: Painted in Death
(Will and Casey-Book 1)
And
Blood and Silence
The Origins of Will Anderson

Devil at Rocky Pointe

Bonus: A Note from Will & Casey

Will: Everyone matters. Every victim. Every clue. Every piece of the puzzle.

Casey: Even when the puzzle looks like Darth Maul after a bad day?

Will: ...Yes. Even then.

Casey: Good. Because somebody has to keep you from going full Jedi-brooding in the corner.

Will: And somebody has to remind you that sarcasm isn't an investigative technique.

Casey: Maybe not. But it gets us through the darkness at light speed.

The Watcher: Light speed burns out fast.

Everyone doesn't matter.

Only the ones chosen do.

And you're already on my board.

Book 3 in the Will Anderson and Casey Murphy Series will continue with **Watcher's Gambit.**

The body was sprawled beneath the clock tower of Ravenwood University, bathed in the yellow wash of campus floodlights. Students clustered behind the police tape, murmuring in the August heat, their whispers carrying the same word over and over: *justice.*

The victim was nineteen: Brock Prescott, A frat boy in the Sigma Epsilon Rho fraternity, still a pledge in the fraternity that calls itself 'The Serpents'. Months earlier, he'd been accused of drugging and assaulting a freshman at a party. The charges evaporated for lack of evidence. Tonight, so had his pulse.

Casey Murphy crouched beside the body, her gloves slick with humidity, jaw set tight. The cause of death was apparent, blunt force trauma. What wasn't obvious sat neatly in the victim's open hand: a single white pawn.

Will Anderson stepped up behind her, his shadow falling over the scene. "Chess piece?" he asked, voice low.

Casey nodded, lifting it with tweezers. "Pawn. Someone left it for us."

Will's frown deepened. "Or for you."

By the time they returned to the precinct, Casey's inbox had already received the first message.

An email. No sender. No signature. Just two sentences:

"The board is set. You are the Rook. Play your part, or more pawns will fall."

Casey stared at the screen, pulse hammering. "They're calling me the Rook."

Will leaned in, his tone steady but grim. "Then this isn't random. Whoever's behind this already knows you."

Casey closed the laptop slowly, but the words burned behind her eyes.

Someone out there was keeping score again.

And this time, the rules weren't written by the Vicar.